Twice Buried

Books by Steven F. Havill

The Posadas County Mysteries
Heartshot
Bitter Recoil
Twice Buried
Before She Dies
Privileged to Kill
Prolonged Exposure
Out of Season
Dead Weight
Bag Limit
Red, Green, or Murder
Scavengers
A Discount for Death
Convenient Disposal
Statute of Limitations
Final Payment
The Fourth Time is Murder

The Dr. Thomas Parks Novels
Race for the Dying
Comes a Time for Burning

Other Novels
The Killer
The Worst Enemy
LeadFire
TimberBlood

Twice Buried

Steven F. Havill

Poisoned Pen Press

First Trade Paperback Edition 2000

10 9 8 7 6 5 4 3 2

Library of Congress Catalog Card Number: 00-102399

ISBN: 978-1-890208-46-2

Poisoned Pen Press
6962 E. First Ave. Ste 103
Scottsdale, AZ 85251
www.poisonedpenpress.com
info@poisonedpenpress.com

Printed in the United States of America

For Kathleen
And a special thanks to Fidel and Leticia Duenas

1

Anna Hocking called the Posadas County sheriff's office at 9:14 P.M. on December 19. That's what the dispatcher said and that's what the telephone log confirmed. That same log showed that I responded to the call at 11:02 P.M. Two hours wasn't our normal response time—but I had a list of excuses as long as my arm. Some of them were even legitimate.

I parked the county car in the narrow driveway that ran through the weeds along the side of Mrs. Hocking's tiny adobe home. Knowing how skittish the old lady could be, I took my time before I got out. I sat in the car with the door ajar and the dome light on, jotting notes on my clipboard.

She would be able to see me easily if she was peering out the window, and she'd know I wasn't some creep intent on robbing her of her riches...which included nothing much more exciting than a thin retirement check and an even thinner Social Security check, both deposited directly to Posadas State Bank.

The porch light wasn't on but the living room light was. Anna Hocking didn't answer my knock. I stepped to one side so that I was in the wash of light flooding out through the multipane window. The lace curtains were thin, ancient, and yellowed, and effectively blocked my view. After the fourth knock, I tried the door. It was locked.

"Mrs. Hocking, it's Bill Gastner," I called. I didn't need to be any more formal than that. She'd known me for years...both my sons and one of my daughters had suffered through English with the old gal during their senior years in high school. My youngest daughter would have endured the experience too if Mrs. Hocking hadn't slipped on the stage during play rehearsal one October night and shattered her hip into a thousand pieces.

I switched on my flashlight and stepped off the porch. The first side window also looked into the living room, but the curtains were drawn and the old-fashioned paper roller shade was pulled as well. The kitchen window, high and narrow over the sink, gave me a slim picture—just enough light filtered in from the living room to make shadows.

The back porch screen door was open and I stepped inside. The porch was full of junk, from firewood that would never be burned to lawn furniture that would never see another barbecue. One window was blocked by a roller blind. Farther down the porch a second one, uncurtained, looked in on a vast inventory of cardboard boxes piled to the ceiling of what once had been a second bedroom.

I frowned. The only other window was on the west side of the house, a single pane of frosted glass that blocked the bathroom's view of the mobile home park next door.

I rapped on the back door, called out my name again, and waited. The house was silent. She hadn't driven anywhere. I knew I'd find Mrs. Hocking's '59 Chrysler in the old garage behind the house, covered by half an inch of dust and bird shit. She hadn't driven the car for ten years.

I rapped again. The door was locked but easy to jimmy. My pocketknife slipped past the striker and the door opened a quarter of an inch, held on the inside by a hook. I popped that and swung the door open.

The house smelled musty, the odor of doilies that had missed their once-a-decade laundering and rugs that had accepted the offerings of a now long-dead terrier when he'd been at his most incontinent. My flashlight beam swept down the short hallway toward the front of the house.

"Mrs. Hocking? It's Bill Gastner. Are you home?"

I stepped into the kitchen and snapped on the overhead light. A colander of unpeeled potatoes rested by the sink. A half-full two-quart bottle of orange juice stood on the counter by the refrigerator. I left the light on and roamed out through the tiny dining room, the living room, the bathroom, and finally the bedroom. The bed was mussed, with the comforter thrown back.

The door of the utility room was ajar and I toed it open.

The smell was faint but unmistakable. "Ah, don't tell me," I said. The utility room, as in most houses, was an overflow room for the daily detritus we all need...soaps, cleansers, brushes, brooms, paints, and a dozen other potions that old lady Hocking had stopped using years before. The hot water heater gurgled gently as it started another cycle. Beside the heater was the door down to the old-fashioned dugout basement. It was half open.

I crossed over, pushed it open the rest of the way, and swept the flashlight beam down the steep, cobweb-laced stairway. The cobwebs danced in the movement of stale air. I stood motionless, listening. Except for the hot water heater, the small adobe house was silent. But the faint odor wafted up from the cellar. I swung the light to the left and the beam's circle collected a pair of feet.

Moving cautiously I bent down until the light could shoot past the floor joists. Mrs. Hocking was crumpled on the dirt floor, her long gray hair about the color of the cellar dust.

Using one hand for support against the wall, I made my way down the stairs. The ancient wood groaned under my weight. That didn't bother me. The cobwebs that floated in the air above my head did, since I didn't know where the black widows were that had spent all that time spinning.

The cellar was tiny, no more than twelve feet square. A hundred years before, the house builders had dug it for the dirt and clay to make the adobe blocks.

On the wall ahead of me were five shelves, their two-by-four supports running from floor to ceiling. The vintage of some of the preserves that lined up soldier straight on the shelves probably ran back to Eisenhower's time.

I knelt down and placed a hand on the old woman's thin neck. Her skin was dry and cool. I shifted my fingers, trying for the pulse that I knew wasn't there. Her eyes were half open, as if she were considering waking up.

There was scarcely space between the stairway and the wall for even a child to curl up but Mrs. Hocking had managed. I stood up.

"What did you do this for, Anna," I said softly. I pulled out my notebook and wrote down the time and a couple of questions

I wanted answered later on. Feeling as if I was invading the privacy of a dignified old friend, I once more swung the flashlight to illuminate the corpse.

Mrs. Hocking was dressed in her pajamas and a pink housecoat, the latter soiled from days of constant use. Both slippers still clung to her small feet. Her lower legs looked like frail bamboo stalks.

Without moving my own feet I turned at the waist, examining the cellar. The beam reflected off a two-cell flashlight that had rolled up against the wall under the shelves. Without touching it, I peered closely. The switch was visible, turned on. The batteries had given up.

Except for Anna Hocking and her flashlight, nothing was out of place. I heaved a sigh, glad that the thousands of students she'd taught over the years didn't have to remember her this way.

Being careful not to disturb anything, I stepped over to the stairway and climbed back upstairs. The telephone was in the living room. I dialed and Gayle Sedillos answered on the second ring.

"Gayle, I need an ambulance out at Anna Hocking's place. And give Emerson Clark a call. Tell him it's an unattended."

My dispatcher said, "Yes sir," and I gave her a couple of seconds to jot notes. She didn't ask questions, knowing full well that I'd fill her in—before just about anyone else—when the time was right.

"And Gayle—"

"Sir?"

"Has Bob Torrez come in yet?"

"Yes, sir. But he's in conference with Glenn Archer."

I cursed my short memory. "Tell 'em to send Archer home. We'll get to him in the morning. Or on Monday. There's nothing we're going to do about that scuffle right now anyway. I need Bob out here."

"Yes, sir."

Archer was the high school principal. He'd grumble that our department was ignoring him again, but I didn't see a round of fisticuffs after a Friday night basketball game as any big deal.

I hung up the phone and glanced at the time. I had about six minutes before Deputy Torrez arrived. Coroner Emerson Clark would be sound asleep, nestled in beside his wife of fifty-eight years, when his telephone rang. He'd be grumpy as hell, but he wouldn't argue with Gayle. He would arrive in less than ten minutes.

I went out on the back porch and sat on one of the window sills, my back against the screen, and waited—and wished that I'd arrived within six minutes of Anna Hocking's last telephone call.

2

Dr. Emerson Clark looked at the stairway and stopped, one hand on each side of the door jamb.

"Oh boy," he muttered. Both Deputy Robert Torrez and I reached out a hand to steady him but he waved us off. "I'm not that goddamned old," he said. He was, but we didn't argue. He went down the stairs one at a time, both hands on the rough wood of the floor joists. I followed. Bob Torrez waited at the head of the stairs, probing through the cobwebs with his flashlight.

"She used this place all these years and never had a damn lightbulb installed," Clark said. He reached the bottom and regarded the tiny, almost doll-like remains of Anna Hocking. "What time did you get here?"

"Shortly after eleven."

Clark used one hand against the dirt cellar wall for support as he lowered himself to his knees. He felt for a pulse, waited several seconds, then took one of Anna Hocking's hands in his. He gently flexed the fingers, then just knelt quietly for a minute.

"She called you?" he asked.

"Yes."

"Was she hearing spooks again?"

"I never asked Gayle. I assumed so."

"What time did she call...not that it's any of my business."

"Shortly after nine."

Clark lifted an eyebrow but otherwise said nothing. He reached out and stroked the thin wisps of hair away from Anna Hocking's neck. His examination was brief. His own fingers were arthritic and beginning to hook, but they were still strong and sure. I'd had confidence in him nineteen years before when he'd taken my oldest son's knee apart and put it back together, and I had no doubts now.

"I'd break into a million pieces too if I were 86 years old and took a tumble like that," he said. "She probably hooked a toe on something. Or maybe a stroke. Autopsy will show."

"There's a loose corner of linoleum right here by the first step," Deputy Torrez said. He still hadn't come down into the basement.

"Well, maybe that's it," Clark said. "I can imagine her hitting the wall there with her head on the way down. That would account for the little scrape on her forehead." He looked at me, expectant.

I held out a hand and this time Clark accepted the help. He came to his feet with a grunt. He turned his own light this way and that, looking around the cellar. "I can think of more comforting places to check out," he said.

"By the time she got down here, it probably didn't matter much," I said.

"There's that," Clark said. He looked down at the corpse again. "I've known her for close to thirty years, Bill. Remember when she broke her hip at school that night?" I nodded. "Bruce Wayland and I worked on her for almost four hours. Hell of a hip job."

He shuffled to the stairway and looked up at Bob Torrez. "You afraid of the dark, son?"

"No, sir," Torrez said. "And sheriff, Linda Rael wants to know if she can come in."

"You've got to be kidding," I said and Clark laughed a dry, short cackle. "She's outside?"

Torrez looked just a trifle uncomfortable. "She rode down with me. She was in the office when you called."

"Then let her sit in the car. This is a private home, for God's sake. Tell the ambulance crew we'll be ready for them as soon as we take a set of pictures." I followed Clark up the stairs and then went outside to fetch the camera kit from the trunk of the car. I glanced down the driveway and saw Linda Rael's dark figure in Torrez's car. The dome light was on. Who knew what she was reading. Probably the deputy's patrol log.

It wasn't until Torrez had mentioned her name that I remembered the letter of permission our county attorney had drawn up so that the young reporter could ride with the deputies on patrol.

None of us knew what Linda and her boss Jim Maestas were after, if anything. She could ride with us until we all retired for all I cared. Sheriff Martin Holman had different ideas, of course. He broke out in goosebumps at the very mention of the media sniffing for anything but the best public relations pieces…those bland, awful things that most county sheriffs released around the holidays.

As undersheriff, I was supposed to sign the letter of permission as well. I hadn't yet, and as far as I knew the document was still buried under mounds of likewise worthless trash on my desk. It was probably right under the newest edition of the department budget—Holman wanted me to read that, too. I would rather have dropped a rock on my foot.

Linda saw me and didn't waste time. It had been thirty years since I could have got out of a car that fast. The ambulance had parked behind Torrez's car and its lights pulsed and bounced off the side of the house.

"Mr. Gastner," Linda Rael called. I set the camera case on the trunk lid and waited. She was a cute kid—maybe twenty-four with a round, dark face framed by one of those old-fashioned pageboy haircuts. I'd read her articles in the *Posadas Register* during the past year or so and she was a competent writer. I'd never noticed her opinions creeping into the stories, even when she was covering one of the deadly county commission meetings. Anyone who could keep a straight face reporting on that nonsense had to have iron will.

"Good evening, Ms. Rael."

"I was going to ask you if I could come inside."

"What changed your mind?" I asked and she looked briefly confused, then smiled.

"I mean, can I come inside?"

I hefted the camera bag. "I don't think so."

"Is the woman dead?"

"Yes." I started toward the back porch door.

"Sir," Linda Rael persisted, and I stopped and turned to face her.

"Look, Linda. Mrs. Hocking was an old woman who lived alone because she chose to do so. She tripped and fell down a flight of stairs. Maybe she had a stroke. But there's no foul play, no crime. It's just an unattended death. The only dignity she has remaining is what we preserve. The public has no rights in there. And we haven't notified any next of kin, so I'd rather that no one was in that house who doesn't need to be."

She didn't argue after that sermon, bless her. Instead she nodded once and said, "I'll wait in the car."

"I'd appreciate that," I said, still surprised to be off the hook so easily. "Were you at the game earlier this evening, by the way?"

She nodded and opened the door of the patrol car. "I got some good shots...some of them were even of basketball." She grinned. Glenn Archer would be at least as nervous as Sheriff Holman. The two of them were a matched pair—public relations paranoids of the first order.

Inside, the two EMT's waited in the living room. "Give us five minutes," I said and went back down in the cellar. I make no claim to be an ace photographer but I burned enough film to make sure I had what I wanted.

Bob Torrez held a flashlight for me while I focused each frame. A full roll of film later, I was satisfied.

In another five minutes the ambulance had left with Anna Hocking's remains.

Upstairs, Torrez and I found what we needed on the first pass. The elderly woman's address book was in the top drawer of an old desk in the living room.

"I'll make a few calls," I said, slipping the book into my shirt pocket. "And by the way, you were out here just last week, weren't you?"

Torrez nodded. "She was hearing noises again, just like before." Anna Hocking's behavior in the past year had drifted toward the irrational as often as not. I had visited her a couple of times myself. All she had wanted was to talk, and when a deputy arrived, she'd have a few minutes of his time.

"I got raspberry that time."

"I beg your pardon?"

Torrez shrugged. "The bribe for coming out for a couple minutes. She gave me a jar of raspberry jam."

I looked at Torrez with amusement. He didn't smile much, but should have. He was one of Posadas County's most eligible bachelors—movie star handsome but so goddamned sober it was funny. I'd once asked him to ride the county float in the Fourth of

July parade, pitching penny candy to the kids along the route. He'd been so straitlaced and forbidding that the kids almost wouldn't run out for the goodies.

"Did she give you something every time you came out?" Torrez's voice was almost inaudible. "Yes, sir."

"She did this with other deputies too?"

"Yes, sir."

My eyes narrowed. "How come I never got anything?"

"I don't know, sir. There's plenty downstairs, though. I'm sure nobody would miss any."

"Spare me," I said. "The Berry Lady," I added. "From now on, buy your own goddamned jam." Torrez almost smiled. "And by the way, I haven't signed the permission letter for Linda Rael to ride with you, so don't get into any trouble before I get back to the office."

"No, sir."

We checked the rest of the house, turning off lights and making sure doors and windows were locked. I put the orange juice back in the refrigerator and for a minute stood there with the door open. The excitement had gone out of Anna Hocking's diet, that was for sure. If I were ever sentenced to live on cottage cheese and fruit juices, I'd probably shoot myself. I shut the refrigerator door.

"Why did she leave the orange juice out?" I asked the deputy. He looked startled, as if he should have an answer.

"Maybe she just forgot it."

"Most likely." We went out on the back porch.

Torrez watched me lock the back door. He didn't ask how I'd gotten in. "Are you making any progress out at Wayne's?"

"I've got a match on one of the footprints," Torrez said. I heard a little pride creep into his voice. Posadas was in the middle of an extended string of penny ante burglaries—all but one of them businesses. The latest hit had been Wayne Farm Supply, three miles southwest of the village on Route 56.

Sheriff Martin Holman had never let us forget where the last residential heist had been. In midsummer his house had burned to the ground. The thieves had thought that a dose of gasoline near the main fuse box would fool the arson investigators. For about five seconds, maybe. The messy fire had disguised the burglary until investigators had really started sifting the ashes. I'd been out of town and missed the show. But I heard about it for weeks when I returned.

Maybe the burglars weren't so dumb. We hadn't caught them yet. I nodded at Torrez. "Super. Show me when we get back."

By the time I walked into my office, it was almost 1:00 A.M. Because it was a quiet winter night, only one deputy was scheduled for the early morning hours. Torrez and I didn't get the chance for any more chitchat. A woman blubbering into the telephone prompted dispatcher Gayle Sedillos to send him out on the family dispute south of town in the Ranchero Trailer Park.

Why a family would dispute at one in the morning was one of life's continuing mysteries. I supposed, knowing the family involved, that hubby had come home when the bars closed, his machismo buoyed by booze. There was no two-hour delay this time. Torrez was on the road while Gayle talked to the woman. Linda Rael rode with the deputy.

I put my feet up on my desk and leafed through Anna Hocking's address book. Her writing, always in black ink, was fine and neat. I found an entry for Frank M. Hocking, 1127 Ventura Place, Bakersfield, California. There was a telephone number, and Mrs. Hocking's son answered on the fifth ring.

I identified myself and broke the news of his mother's death. He was not surprised and sounded more resigned than anything else. He asked for the name and number of a funeral home and I gave him a choice of two. He picked Teddy Salazar's Family Mortuary. All in all, Frank and I wrapped up the remains of Anna Hocking's long life efficiently and politely.

At 1:17 A.M., I left the office for home with a reminder for Gayle that I wanted to be called if anything serious cropped up. Torrez's being the only cop on the road didn't bother me. The reporter in the passenger seat did.

When I stretched out in bed, my eyelids felt like lead. Maybe I'd be able to catch some regular sleep after all. I sighed and rolled over, my thoughts drifting south of the border.

I had seven days before I left for the tiny village of Tres Santos in Mexico where my godson was to be christened. Estelle Reyes-Guzman and her husband Francis had named me *padrino* for the little wrinkled kid, an honor I couldn't take lightly. Estelle had been my best deputy—and then she'd moved north when Francis took a position with the Public Health Service.

We kept in close touch—I was practically as much family to them as Estelle's aging mother in Tres Santos or her infamous great-uncle Reuben in Posadas. I was looking forward to their visit south for the ceremony in old Mexico.

The pleasant mental excursion away from the terminal disease of law enforcement didn't last long. Some stupid synapse deep in my brain triggered itself. My eyes snapped open. Like a video playing in my mind, I saw the staircase down into Anna Hocking's fruit cellar and the cobwebs floating in the musty air currents.

I turned over and stared at the ceiling. That was no better. I pulled myself out of bed and in ten minutes was backing the county car out of my driveway. I almost radioed Bob Torrez but then thought better of it. As I drove through the village there was no traffic. The Christmas decorations in the plaza and along Bustos Avenue were sparse. The lighted candy canes didn't do much to make Posadas look less desolate.

It was a hell of a time to go calling, but Anna Hocking's ghost wouldn't care.

3

Anna Hocking's little adobe house on County Road 19 was waiting for me...at least that's the way it seemed. I drove out Bustos Avenue, now dark except for the sea of lights that illuminated the new car lot around Chavez Chevrolet-Olds. Across the road, Hamburger Heaven had been out of business now for almost two years, and just beyond the joint's remains I turned onto County Road 19. Inside the village, the street was called Camino del Sol. At the county line, it lost that pretension.

The macadam turned to dirt with gravel kicked to the shoulders, roller-coastering through a series of dips and tight curves as it avoided the worst of Arroyo del Cerdo. When a summer flood in 1952 had turned the arroyo into a raging, crashing torrent, the brown tide took away most of Ellis Pacheco's pig farm, carrying the squealers right into town where their bloated corpses decorated the town square.

If nothing else, the storm produced a name for the arroyo. And Ellis didn't learn. He rebuilt his pens within a few feet of the newly cut arroyo edge.

At the top of a rise, I drove quietly past Valerio's Mobile Home Park. When Consolidated Mining decided Posadas wasn't worth another stick of dynamite, they shut down their copper pit without warning, putting 460 miners on the dole. Within a month, most of the miners had left for richer ore bodies. Trailers left parks like water through a busted dam. Valerio's was down to the last three residents. A single sodium vapor light glared harshly at the entrance. Despite the December chill, I buzzed the window down. The place was dark and silent.

On the opposite side of the road were two acres of ministorage barns, empty for years and starting to crumble. A local contractor owned them and showed no interest in doing anything other than letting the property molder.

Just beyond the great blotchy plywood sail that had been a drive-in movie screen was another mobile home park. The berms of the drive-in, minus speaker poles, were all that remained of the former and a few bent and twisted utility boxes marked the remains of the park.

At one time, this end of Posadas had been bustling, growing so fast that folks were even talking about a mall. Now, not much holiday cheer radiated out Camino del Sol.

I passed an abandoned wrecking yard and yet a third mobile home park on the left. Two trailers remained there, both dark and silent. I saw one car in the driveway of Miriam Sloan's trailer. Over the years the tires of Posadas County Sheriff's Department cars had about worn arroyos to her door, cursed as she was with a little heller for a son and a boyfriend who had cornered the market on stupidity.

Finally, half hidden under elms gone to twig and brush, was Anna Hocking's place.

I drove slowly past. Sixty-five years ago, before the junk moved in to fester along the county road right to this front doorstep, the tiny adobe had graced the bunch grass hills as headquarters for the Hocking ranch.

Abe Hocking's place was nearly a thousand acres and four miles from the Posadas Village Square. He'd talked Anna Guilcrest into marrying him, sired a couple children, raised some of the finest Hereford stock in the southwest, and even talked about building a bigger, grander house up the arroyo a thousand yards near the summer shade of the mesa.

One summer evening in 1942, Abe Hocking sipped a little too much mescal, a drink of which he was inordinately fond, and drove his 1936 Ford pickup into the arroyo just about where the turnoff to the drive-in theater now scarred the sand. The truck wasn't too banged up, but Abe's window had been open and he was partly in and partly out when the truck rolled the second time. The young widow took up school teaching that fall and didn't retire until 1979.

A half mile beyond the Hocking place I slowed, found a wide spot in the road and turned around. I switched off the headlights and let the Ford idle back down the road. A hundred yards from the adobe I stopped, buzzed down the passenger side windows, and turned off the engine.

In the distance a dog yipped and then fell silent. A mile southeast of Posadas and three miles from where I had parked, the interstate exchange was a sea of bright yellow vapor lights. I could see the running lights of trucks on the highway, but the breeze carried their constant drone away from me.

Anna Hocking's house was a dark lump against the night sky, featureless and empty. After ten minutes I started the car and let it idle along the gravel. I didn't pull into the driveway. When I got out of the car the December night was cold enough to make me wish I'd worn a heavier coat. I took my briefcase and flashlight and walked to the back porch.

This time when I jimmied the back door I let it swing open and didn't enter. My flashlight beam shot down the narrow hallway and I could see into the kitchen to the left. I knelt and with the flashlight an inch from the linoleum let the beam sweep the hallway floor. The old vinyl was clean except for the dust filigree along the baseboards.

I ignored the kitchen and went to the utility room, turning on the ceiling light as I entered. The door to the cellar was closed tight, just as Bob Torrez and I had left it. I turned the knob and pulled it open. The same musty smell greeted me. With care I reached up and touched one of the cobwebs. I knew that some spiders, particularly house spiders and widows, were sloppy web spinners. These webs were both sloppy and profuse. A thick strand floated next to the wall on the right side of the stairwell, attached only to one of the ceiling rafters.

With care I walked down the stairs and stopped at the bottom. The cellar floor was dirt and our bootprints were clear. I counted four sets…mine, Emerson Clark's, and the two EMT's. None belonged to Anna Hocking. When she'd hit the floor she was either dead or too hurt to move.

I turned, examining the floor. There were no other footprints. I frowned. I wanted a photograph of the cellar floor but I was rapidly reaching the limit of my photographic expertise. Leaving the manual 35mm in the briefcase, I selected the little instant camera with auto everything. I held it down low, no more than a foot off the floor, and shot obliquely across the cellar. Maybe the wash of the flash would highlight the slight impressions left behind by the foot traffic.

I took several photos, including a series of the dust-covered jars on the shelves, then concentrated on the stairs and stairwell. Again the cobwebs fascinated me. None of them hung down low enough to touch Anna Hocking on the head had she been standing on the stairs at that moment. They hadn't touched me either…and at five feet ten inches I was a head taller than Mrs. Hocking.

Having finished the roll of film I climbed back up to the utility room. I placed my briefcase on the washing machine, turned around, and folded my arms, leaning against the machine.

My pulse was beating a little faster but not because of exertion. I was trying to formulate some answers to impossible questions when I heard a car pull into the driveway. I stretched over and quickly flicked off the utility room light, the only one I had turned on.

Walking to the kitchen as lightly as my considerable girth would allow, I looked out the window. The low burble of the exhausts was familiar. When Bob Torrez opened the door of his patrol car I heard him say quietly, "You better stay there."

I relaxed and went to meet the deputy at the back door, first turning on the utility room light again so it flooded out into the hallway.

Torrez grinned when he saw me. "Couldn't sleep, sir?"

"No. And how'd you know I was here?"

"We were just cruising back up this way. We saw your car."

"Come on in. I've got a couple of questions to ask you."

Torrez closed the screen door behind him. "About what, sir?" he asked as he followed me back to the utility room.

"You said you were out here last week?"

"That's right."

"When the two of you were finished talking about ghosts and she offered you the jar of jam, did she already have it upstairs? Or did she go down and get it?"

Torrez shook his head and looked at me, puzzled. "I went down and got it."

"You did."

"Yes, sir."

"Show me."

"What do you mean?"

"Show me what you did. Do just what you did last week."

The deputy glanced at the door to the cellar. "Well, I just walked over here—"

"Where was she?"

"In the living room. She didn't get up out of her chair, even. She said she was feeling a little lame."

"And you knew right where the cellar door was?"

"Yes. I've been here before."

"Ever been down in the cellar before?"

Torrez shook his head. "No. But I fixed her washing machine for her once." He saw the expression on my face and said quickly, "It was just leaking a little from the hot water fitting. I just tightened it. While I was doing that, she went down and got a jar."

"You saw her do that?"

"Sure. But that was six months ago or so. She was getting around better then."

"All right." I gestured at the door. "Show me."

He opened the cellar door and hesitated. "I hate these things," he said, so quietly I almost didn't hear him. He ducked down low, flinching away from the cobwebs. When he was halfway down the stairs I told him to stop. He did so, still scrunched. He turned his head to look back at me.

"Is that the way you went down there last week?"

"What do you mean?"

"All hunched over like that."

He nodded.

"Don't like spiders much?"

He made a face. The nearest web was almost three feet over his head.

"Go on down." I followed him into the cellar. "Anything changed?"

He scanned the shelves and the jars and then shook his head. "No. You can see where the jar was that I took."

"Uh-huh. Did you happen to notice the floor when you were down here?"

"No." This time he did glance down.

"That's one reason I came back out here. There were four sets of footprints in this nice, fine dust." I knelt down and rubbed some of the dirt between my fingers. "Mine, Clark's, and the two ambulance attendants." Bob Torrez looked sideways at me. "And none of your size thirteens. You see how visible they are in places? You didn't come down here earlier tonight." I smiled. "And now I know why. *Las arañas* aren't your favorite beasties, are they?"

He grinned sheepishly.

"But now tell me why your bootprints aren't here from a week ago."

When he was finished examining the dirt floor, he sat back on his haunches. "I don't know, sir. Maybe she swept the place since then."

"You don't believe that and neither do I. Someone who doesn't bother to dust off food storage jars isn't going to bother with a dirt floor."

"Maybe she's got one of those volunteers from the Department of Human Services who does cleaning."

"Sure. Including sweeping a dirt fruit cellar floor? I don't think so."

"What are you thinking, sir?"

"I don't know. At first I got to wondering about the cobwebs. I didn't have to sweep them aside. I figured that you did that a few days ago. But after I saw your performance just now—"

"They were practically in my face last week."

"Yeah, but your face is about two feet higher than Anna Hocking's."

"Maybe she flailed her arms as she was falling."

"Flail, Robert? She was eighty-six years old. I can't picture it."

"You're saying that someone swept the tracks smooth? Even took a sweep at the cobwebs?"

"Maybe."

"The doors weren't locked and latched when you first came?"

"Yes," I said, then thought better of it. "The ones that I checked were."

Torrez looked toward the staircase. His right hand rested unconsciously on the butt of his service automatic.

"If someone was here and wanted Mrs. Hocking's death to look like an accident, the doors would all have to be locked. From the inside. But there would have to be a way of getting out."

We both went back upstairs. Old houses hide some secrets pretty well. But it's just about impossible to make modern tampering blend in. Whoever had painted the inside of Anna Hocking's windows years before had been sloppy. The three living room windows were painted shut—and locked.

The kitchen window was solid. So was the bedroom window.

"She wasn't one for fresh air, was she?" Torrez said.

"A lot of elderly folks aren't," I said. We went to the bathroom. Only a ferret could have squeezed through the two inches that the rusty casement hardware allowed.

"I don't think so," the deputy said. We opened the door to the second bedroom. Mrs. Hocking had saved every cardboard box for the last decade. There was a path of sorts and I made my way to the window that looked out onto the back porch.

It hadn't been painted shut. The brass swivel lock in the top center of the lower window's frame was open.

"You think they went out this way?"

"Maybe. Don't touch anything until you've dusted for prints. Then we'll see how easily it moves."

"If someone came here, she must have let them in."

"Unless they jimmied the door as easily as I did earlier."

"And then went out this way? I'm not sure I buy the cellar idea, sir," Torrez said. "I mean, there's a dozen ways that footprints can get obliterated. And the ones that we could see weren't all that clear."

I shrugged and ran a hand across the bristle brush of my gray hair. "Why don't you get the print kit. Then we'll see."

My intuition told me I was right even if nothing else did. While Torrez went outside, I returned to the utility room. A broom was standing in the corner, almost behind the hot water heater. Farther back in the corner was an old dust mop that looked like one of those long-haired oriental dogs without legs.

I spread a black trash bag on the floor and then, using a paper towel, gently picked up the broom by the end of the handle. I held it two feet over the black plastic and dropped it straight down. Nothing. I made a face and put the broom away.

Just as carefully, I leaned around the heater, picked up the dust mop and repeated the performance. This time, when it hit the plastic, a fine spray of adobe brown dirt formed a halo around the mop.

"Gotcha, you son of a bitch," I muttered.

4

By ten the next morning, we had a fair-sized convocation at Anna Hocking's. It was too bad that she had to be dead to receive all that attention.

I hadn't minded the long hours. I could recharge my batteries with a couple minutes of sleep a night. If I got that much I considered myself lucky. But Linda Rael, the young reporter, was among the walking dead. The dark circles under her eyes made her look like she'd been popped twice by an angry boyfriend.

By dawn, Linda was content just to sit in the car, bravely trying not to let her eyelids crash shut. I still refused to let her into the house. The last time we'd talked, her temper was beginning to fray. That made Sheriff Martin Holman nervous. To him, nothing was worse than angry press.

"I think we're about finished, don't you?" he asked. He'd cornered me on the back porch, about as close to the inside as I'd let him go. He never seemed to know what to touch and what to leave the hell alone.

"Eddie Mitchell is still dusting for prints in the kitchen. When he's finished there, we can concentrate on finishing up outside."

Holman gazed out through the porch screen at the yellow crime scene ribbon that circled the little house—and that included the driveway and the yard. Deputy Tony Abeyta, two months on the force and scheduled to begin academy training the next week, strolled around that circle, eyes watchful. So far, Linda Rael was the only newshound present, but as the word got out others would show up.

Sheriff Holman was unimpressed with my theories. As more of a tip of the hat to his office than his person, I'd taken him down into the cellar briefly and explained what I thought had happened. Holman was no cop—he'd sold used cars before his election first to the county commission and then later as sheriff—but he was smarter than I usually gave him credit for being.

He did have a perfect talent for knowing what to say to the media.

"I can't tell Linda that we think we've got a murder because of some cobwebs and a little dust on a mop."

"I can understand that," I said.

"I mean, brooms and dustmops are *supposed* to have dirt on them."

"Uh-huh. The lab's going to tell us that the dirt on that mop came from the cellar floor."

Holman looked pained. "Come on, Bill. This whole hillside is the same dirt. You sweep the living room floor and you get that dirt."

I shook my head and fumbled for a cigarette. The pocket was empty. "Nope. That would be blow sand…or light blow dirt. This is old adobe dust, the kind of stuff that sifts gently over the years. Fine as silt."

"So she swept her cellar."

I shook my head again. "She hasn't even been able to go down in the cellar for months."

"And you've found no other evidence?"

"No. Just the mop, the lack of footprints, the disturbed cobwebs, and the open back window."

Holman took three steps to his right and looked at the offending window. "That's probably been open for years, Bill."

"Probably."

He was about to say something else when Robert Torrez walked quickly along the side of the house to the back porch.

"Sir," he said, "Gayle wants you to call her."

"Right now?"

"She said it was important."

"Excuse me, Martin."

"And speaking of calls, Glenn Archer called me early this morning," Sheriff Holman said.

"I'll bet he did."

"He wasn't too happy."

"I'll bet he wasn't," I said and went inside the house to use the old black telephone in the living room.

The dispatcher answered on the second ring. I said, "What's up, Gayle?"

"Sir, Carla Champlin called." I groaned. I didn't want to see Carla Champlin that morning, any more than I wanted to see Glenn Archer. "She wants to talk to you, sir."

"What about, did she say?"

"She wouldn't tell me much, sir. She just said that I should tell you that she wants to file a complaint against an old friend of yours."

"An old friend of mine?"

"That's what she said, sir."

"When did she call?"

"About four minutes ago."

"And she didn't want anyone else?"

"No, sir. She said you'd know just what she meant."

"I don't know what she means. But call her back and tell her I'll be there as soon as I can."

I hung up and turned to see Martin Holman inspecting one of the living room windows. He was running his finger along the middle framework as if he were a butler checking for dust instead of ruining prints, which is what he was doing.

"Problems?" he asked.

"I don't know. Carla Champlin wants me for something."

"Lucky you."

I grunted and glanced at my watch. My first inclination was to put Ms. Champlin on hold. But I knew that Bob Torrez was competent. He and the other officers would finish up. I could trust them to be careful and thorough. I glanced at my watch again. The night before, I'd let two hours slide by after Anna Hocking's call when five minutes might have made a vital difference to the old woman.

"If anyone needs me, I'll be at the post office," I said.

5

The post office was a low, dark adobe building tucked between two other drab businesses on the west side of the village square.

On that Saturday morning, the square was quiet and dusty. Dusty in December. That was Posadas's claim to fame. It was warm enough even with the low winter sun that someone could have been relaxing in the old gazebo centered in the square. No one was.

Come evening, the village crews would light the Christmas *luminarias* around the park. The candles closed in brown paper bags would cheer the place up a little, their flickering light dancing up through the bare, sere branches of the elms. Cheerful, unless some of the antsy high school kids kicked the bags over and set the park on fire.

Posadas, New Mexico, wasn't high on the list as a setting for a holiday TV special. It would take a hell of a set of camera filters to put color in the place. The even, monotonous tan of sand stretched off to the horizon in all directions. Even the mesas were tan except during those few moments each day when the setting sun swept them with rose hues.

Other towns had Indian pueblos nearby for color and commerce... not Posadas. It was cheaper to go souvenir shopping in old Mexico, just twenty miles south. There were no lakes to lend sparkle to the place, unless you counted the abandoned and groundwater-filled quarry behind Consolidated Mining up on the mesa.

But we weren't entirely without attractions. The year before, a group of spelunkers had convinced the Bureau of Land Management that a series of caves in the small lava flow west of town was worthy of federal interest. In twenty years, Martinez's Tube, as we called it, might be elevated to tourist-trap status. No one was holding his breath.

The post office was as quiet as the rest of the town. I entered the cool building and smelled the antiseptic detergent with which Carla Champlin scoured every surface several times a week. I looked around the tiny foyer.

Four strands of tinsel crisscrossed the lobby with little foil stars swinging below. A pile of unwanted mail-order catalogs weighted down one end of the courtesy counter. I leaned on the window shelf.

"Just one moment," a high, thin voice warbled from the back room.

"No hurry, Carla," I called. "It's Bill Gastner."

She appeared carrying her right arm outstretched toward me as if she wanted to shake hands from twenty feet away. "Catalogs," she said, and cast eyes heavenward.

"Catalogs?"

"Oh, you wouldn't believe it. I think every boxholder in Posadas County receives five thousand catalogs. *Big* ones. As if the usual holiday package rush wasn't enough."

She pushed a strand of steely gray hair back under a hairpin. Her head was narrow and her face angular. The Postal Service blouse hung over a bony body. I always thought that hugging Carla Champlin would be like fondling a bundle of construction rebar. She was three years older than me, but a hands-down winner if the two of us were ever paired in a physical contest.

"Uh-huh," I said, for want of anything more sympathetic. I pushed my Stetson back and rubbed my forehead and the stubble of gray hair above. "Gayle Sedillos said you needed to see me about something?"

Carla Champlin leaned out the window and eyed the vacant little lobby with all its polished brass-doored boxes. "Is it true what I heard about Anna Hocking?"

"That she died last night? Yes, that's true." The efficiency of the Posadas grapevine was astounding.

Carla looked at me hard for a minute, then said, "Such a dear, dear lady."

"Yes, ma'am. She was a wonderful person."

"Last night, wasn't it?"

"Yes."

She tsk-tsked and then leaned a little farther out the window. I almost backpedaled a step, thinking she was going to grab me. But I stood my ground, both hands on the window sill.

"Sheriff, now listen." She began as if my attention might stray. Her perfume was stout. And I wasn't the sheriff of Posadas County. I was undersheriff, one of those awkward titles that the public can't manage.

"Gayle said you had a complaint."

Her eyebrows knitted together. If I cut short her story, she would be really pissed.

"Sheriff, now, you know," and she accented *know* as if the word were biblical in its authority, "that it is a violation of federal law to carry a weapon on post office property."

"Yes ma'am."

"A violation of *federal* law," she repeated. To her, federal law and Moses' commandments were carved from the same clay.

"Sure."

"Unless you're a law officer."

"That's right."

"Well, you certainly know Mr. Reuben Fuentes." She wrinkled her slim nose. Her lips pursed. Maybe she was planning to whistle "White Christmas."

"Indeed I do. He was carrying a firearm?" I hated to cut short the pleasure of her storytelling, but I had work to do. And then maybe a serious nap to take.

"Well, now, he came in here shortly after nine...I was just finishing sorting. He is so crippled that it took him nearly five minutes just to cross to this counter. And that's when I saw it. He had this enormous holster on his belt. And of course I could see the gun in it."

Reuben Fuentes had been carrying a weapon of one kind or another since he was six years old. "Yes, ma'am," I said patiently.

"He's worn it in here before and I've never said anything." She lifted her chin, proud of her generosity. "But *this* time—"

"Tell me what happened."

She leaned forward and lowered her voice. "He came to the counter here and asked to purchase five stamps. I took the stamps from the drawer. He hung his cane on the counter lip and fumbled in his pocket for money."

"His cane?" I'd never seen Reuben with a cane, drunk or sober.

"Indeed. He fumbled for his money and then he discovered it was in the pocket covered by the gun and holster." She pantomimed Reuben's absentminded fumbling.

I raised an eyebrow and waited for the punch line with a straight, official face.

"Sheriff, he pulled out that monstrous revolver and laid it right *here* on the counter! I could look right down the barrel. And I could see the ends of the bullets."

"He took the gun out of the holster?"

"He did. And then he rummaged around until he found his coin purse. He paid me for the stamps and put the purse back in his pocket."

"And then he put the gun away and left?"

"He did no such thing. You know Ella Fernandez? Well, at that moment she came in with her ailing mother. Mr. Fuentes picked up the revolver—I assume to put it away—and dropped it! Can you imagine that? He dropped it, Sheriff. I thought Mrs. Fernandez was going to have heart failure."

"I'm sure."

"Well. He's so crippled. He hung onto the counter with one hand and bent down, trying to pick up the gun. I thought he was surely going to fall. Finally, Ella reached down and picked it up. He mumbled something when she handed it to him. Then he left. And *that* took another five minutes."

"I see."

"Now, Sheriff, that thing might have gone off and killed someone."

"Yes, ma'am."

"I told Ella and her mother that I would talk to you. I've heard that you know Mr. Fuentes rather well. I can't overemphasize how important this is, Sheriff. It is my responsibility to make sure that nothing like this happens again."

"You did the right thing."

She softened a little. "I mean, don't misunderstand me. I wouldn't want Mr. Fuentes arrested or anything like that. But you must make him understand, Sheriff. And you know—" she leaned forward again and whispered, "he drinks *so much*."

"Yes, ma'am." I pushed away from the counter and straightened up. "I'll run out and have a chat with him. And thanks for giving me the call. I appreciate it."

"Thank you, Sheriff." She smiled. She needed new dentures. "I have some coffee on in back if you'd care for some."

"No, thanks. I had too much for breakfast." I nodded and did my best to look solemnly official. "I'll talk to Reuben and let you know."

The sun was bright through the few skeletal elms when I walked outside. I sat in the county car for a minute, drumming my fingers on the steering wheel.

Now that I thought about it, I couldn't remember when I'd seen Reuben Fuentes with a gun in recent months, or even years. A week before, I'd seen him hobbling up and down the aisles of Griego's Big G Supermart. He hadn't been using a cane then. And he hadn't been carrying a gun.

Two weeks before that, he'd driven his battered Bronco into a bar ditch. Deputy Eddie Mitchell had turned the front hubs, yanked the old truck into four-wheel drive, and then rocked it free. The deputy said old Reuben hadn't been drunk that day, or he wouldn't have let him plod on homeward. Eddie was a methodical, thorough young cop. If Reuben Fuentes had been wearing a gun, the deputy would have mentioned it in his report.

I accelerated the county car away from the curb and headed toward the west edge of town. It wouldn't take long to swing out past Reuben's place and have a chat.

I owed him a visit anyway, to make sure that he hadn't forgotten that he was going with me to his great-grandnephew's christening. He probably wouldn't remember the incident in the post office. He could recall everything about the summer of 1916 and nothing about an hour ago.

Reuben Fuentes, in his lilting and fractured Mexican-English, could describe the great Pancho Villa better than any photograph. But about himself, Reuben was not reliable. He was either 84, 96, or 101, depending on when he was asked. He was oldest when he was ailing—as most of us are. He was youngest when wrapped around a bottle of Black Velvet.

His stories over the years had blended into a wonderful hodge-podge of fact laced liberally with whimsy. His grandniece and my former deputy, Estelle Reyes-Guzman, had said that old Reuben was born in 1898. She treasured a yellowed and brittle newspaper clipping from 1899 about a rubella outbreak. That story mentioned the infant Reuben as one of the fatalities. Even then, the media got their facts screwed up.

As I drove through town, I reflected that getting the old man to travel south for his great-grandnephew's christening was going to be a considerable challenge. Riding in a car with him for even those few miles was going to be worse.

I frowned, curious now why a ninety-four-year-old man had started packing his iron again.

6

Reuben Fuentes lived eleven miles west of Posadas. If Carla Champlin had called my office as soon as the old man had left the post office, then I was only fifteen minutes behind him. I'd seen him drive before, inching his old Bronco along the county roads as if it were an overloaded, fragile buggy. Fourth gear in that truck was damn near virgin.

By the time I turned off State Road 17, trading the smooth macadam for thick gravel with rocks the size of baseballs, I had already let my mind wander. Sheriff Martin Holman was probably right to be skeptical. Pure mental gymnastics had concocted the entire Hocking affair.

Over the years I'd seen circumstances far more suspicious or even bizarre surrounding what turned out to be an innocent accident. Hell, one icy January several years before, we'd spent two days looking for the car that had smacked old Efren Padilla while he was walking along the county road in front of his ramshackle place south of town.

He'd been found by another motorist, bleeding profusely, his scalp all but torn off the right side of his head. His right arm was snapped in two places. For a few hours the emergency room doctor at Posadas General had had his hands full trying to keep Efren alive.

We'd been so pissed that someone would run down an old drunk that we'd damn near torn the county apart looking for a vehicle with fresh damage to the front end.

And then, after about fifty hours, Efren had regained consciousness and embarrassed the hell out of all of us.

He had decided in the dark of night, he told us, that he wanted to have a talk with his horse. He had stumbled from the house nearly blind drunk and made his way to the little barn and corral. The horse hadn't shared his enthusiasm for nighttime conversation and had kicked old Efren in the side of the head. The iron horseshoe had laid open the old man's scalp from eyebrow to crown.

Efren had fallen, yelling like a madman. His cries had spooked the horse and a thousand pounds of animal danced sideways, planting first one hoof and then another on Efren's arm. The bone snapped like a dry twig.

Efren told us that after that he didn't remember much. He could vaguely recall stumbling back toward the house. Where he had actually stumbled was in the opposite direction. He collapsed on the shoulder of the highway, leaving it to the rest of us to assume the worst.

In all likelihood, it had been even simpler for Anna Hocking. We'd found no hint of burglary, no hint of argument, no trace of a struggle. It had to be simple.

She'd decided to check out the basement for whatever reason, stubbed an old toe on a torn fragment of linoleum, and pitched forward into blackness. That simple. The unlatched window no doubt had been unlatched since summer.

I slowed the county car for the first of several cattle guards and gritted my teeth as the wheels jounced across. I glanced to my right at the first of what would be dozens of For Sale signs that Stuart Torkelson Realty had posted in the overgrazed pasture to the north.

"Live in Rural Beauty" the signs promised. I grinned. Arid beauty, maybe. No electricity. No plumbing. No driveways. *No nada.* Torker had proven over the years he could sell anything to almost anybody. This patch of desert was going to challenge even his skills.

Maybe he knew something about the potential of Martinez's Tube that none of the rest of us did. Carlsbad Caverns they weren't, but maybe Torkelson had vision. Maybe folks from back east really would flock to clamber down inside 600 feet of cold, dank, black rock.

But my mind wasn't concerned with real estate investments. Instead, it continued to play the Hocking tape. There had to be a simple reason why Deputy Bob Torrez's bootprints had been obliterated from Mrs. Hocking's cellar floor. Maybe she'd decided to sell the place and had cleaned it up—or had it cleaned up—before the realtor visited. Or maybe the circumstances just weren't right for obvious prints. Maybe the dirt of the cellar floor was as hard as only hundred-year old dirt could be, impervious to scuff marks and imprints.

I hit the second cattle guard too fast and the front end of the Ford bottomed out with a crash. I swore and slowed to a crawl. The dust from the road filtered into the car, a sweet musty smell, and I turned on the air conditioner.

Two more cattle guards and a blue sea of For Sale signs paraded by before I reached the turnoff to Reuben Fuentes's ranch. His driveway made the gravel county road seem like an interstate. The wheelbase of the patrol car was too wide for the ruts and the Ford jounced and scraped as I followed the lane toward a jutting brow of limestone.

For more than forty years, old man Fuentes had lived hard-scrabble on this property. He'd probably enjoyed every minute of it. Or so he'd always said. His wife, Rosa, had never professed any love for the dry, piñon- and juniper-studded land. She'd finally given up and died on Reuben's eightieth birthday.

Even Estelle Reyes-Guzman had given up trying to convince the old man to move into the twentieth century. The small stone house came into view as I wound the county car through a dense grove of juniper and crashed across a dry wash.

Nailed to a stout pinon tree in the front yard was a No Traspessing sign, its misspelling bleached with age.

I doubted if Reuben had had a trespasser, no matter how it was spelled, in thirty years, barring the occasional deer hunter who strayed off course. One of the popular Posadas County rumors had the old man's notches counting six men killed over the years. I knew of two.

When he was thirty-seven years old and living in the little Mexican village of Tres Santos with his sister, he'd been caught up in a dispute with three other men over ownership of half a dozen bag-of-bones cattle.

Somehow—the years had bleached those facts too—the dispute turned nasty. Reuben had been quicker and luckier. One of the men had pulled a little .32 topbreak revolver and Reuben had grabbed it away from him. The first little pellet had hit Simon Vasquez right between the eyes. Simon's brother Juan and a cousin sprinted for their lives toward their wagon. Reuben jerked the trigger until the gun was empty.

All but one of those four shots buried themselves harmlessly in the Mexican sand. The third slug raked along the top of the wagon seat and then buried itself in Juan's left kidney.

When Estelle's mother—Reuben's niece—told me what she knew of the episode, she maintained that Juan Vasquez lived for almost a week.

That was enough time for every member of the Vasquez family, and they were legion, to gather weapons and set out after Reuben. Reuben was no fool. He decided that United States citizenship was just the ticket.

It was altogether possible, though, that after all those years he still kept one rheumy eye cocked toward the timber, waiting for the Vasquez boys to show up.

The versions of that story had flourished, of course, growing and vitalizing over the years. Reuben had kept the old .32 revolver. That weapon or some other had been at his side for half a century, until he was too old to remember how the holster was supposed to fit on his belt. Over the years, he'd acquired guns of one kind or another by the dozens.

Local color, the Posadas Chamber of Commerce nervously called him. He was that, unshaven, unwashed, with his felt hat pulled low over his eyes, and more often than not mumbling to himself in Mexican.

But he'd never shot anyone else as far as I knew. Five or six years before, he'd said he'd come damn close when a couple of Jehovah's Witnesses took him on as a project. It was his driveway rather than his artillery that had discouraged them in the end.

Reuben Fuentes's cabin was twenty-four feet on a side. The flat roof was traditional rock and dirt on logs and latillas. When it leaked badly in strategic spots, he'd made repairs with black plastic weighted down with discarded tires.

I parked near the remains of a '48 GMC pickup truck and got out of the county car. An archaeologist was going to have a lark when he excavated Reuben's front yard in a thousand years.

Nothing had gone to the county landfill. When he'd somehow accidentally punched a hole in his washbasin in 1952, he hadn't thrown it away. He took an ice pick and punched a couple dozen more holes. He'd used the thing as a bean colander until the rust flakes showed up in his stew. *Then* the blue porcelain had been flung outside to rest with everything else…the old shoes, the busted axe handle, the myriad tin cans, the GMC and four of its cousins, the other washbasins from other decades.

The place was quiet. Reuben's '73 Ford Bronco was parked beside the cabin, nestled between an old school bus and what had probably been a chicken coop. I made my way to the door, ready for the chorus of barks from Reuben's three mutts.

I hesitated, listening. The hasp wasn't closed where Reuben normally hung his padlock but the slab-wood door was pulled tightly shut. I knocked and waited.

"Reuben!" I called. Whatever ailments the old man suffered, deafness hadn't been one of them. I rapped again. "Reuben! It's Bill Gastner." I turned and surveyed the yard and surrounding trees. The dogs would have greeted me if they'd seen or heard me. I stepped away from the cabin and walked along the cluttered two-track that led past the Bronco.

The vehicle's hood was warm, but not more than the hot sun would bake it. I took a deep breath, wishing I had something other than the aroma from fragrant juniper needles for refreshment. I set off down the two-track toward the pastures.

Fifty yards beyond the cabin I reached the first barbed wire fence and stopped. To my left, the fence gate was open. I squinted into the sun. Ahead of me was a thousand acres of rough country where Reuben had once pastured his cattle. As far as I knew, he didn't own a single steer anymore.

I was damned if I was going to hike the countryside looking for the old man. He was probably sitting in the shade of a piñon somewhere, smoking his pipe, pulling on a whiskey bottle, and watching me.

I turned and started to walk back to the cabin. I hadn't taken ten steps when I saw him, one hand outstretched to rest against the rough stones of the cabin wall. He waited in the shade as I approached.

"Good morning, Reuben," I said. Almost in slow motion, he released his grip on the wall of the house. I wasn't sure that he recognized me. He turned his head slightly and I pushed my Stetson back on my head so the brim didn't shadow my face.

"*Señor,*" he said. "*¿Cuando va a venir Estelita?*"

I relaxed a little. That was his standard question on those dozen or so occasions each year when I spoke with him. His grandniece had spent considerable time with Reuben, especially after Rosa's death. The old man had been one of Estelle's major worries when she'd accepted a job with a sheriff's department up in the northern part of the state. It had been her mother who had finally convinced her to leave Posadas...and convinced her that the old man would do just fine without her. And he had.

I smiled at him. "*La semana próxima,*" I said, exhausting most of my abilities to speak Mexican. Estelle was *not* coming that next week. Reuben had forgotten that we were driving south for the christening of Estelle's first child.

The old man muttered something I didn't catch and waved a hand as he turned to go back inside. As he turned, I saw that he was still wearing the revolver. And it wasn't a little .32 topbreak, either. I could see enough of it to recognize the heavy Colt Single Action.

He shuffled to the door and pushed it open. The bottom edge scraped along an arc worn in the wooden floor. The door hadn't fit properly when he'd hung it and hadn't improved with time.

Inside, the little cabin was the deep cool that only stone houses offer. That was the extent of the amenities. The place stank—a rich, permeating, choking potpourri of odors that would take a week to categorize and isolate. The dogs were no doubt responsible for much of it. Judging by the thick tapestry of pet hair that clung to every fabric surface, the animals owned the place.

I took another step farther inside as Reuben shuffled toward the ancient round-top refrigerator. The cabin was dimly lit, its clutter mercifully hidden by shadows. Dominating the far wall was a massive stone fireplace whose mantel had been hewn from an alligator bark juniper log sixteen inches in diameter that Reuben had pulled down off the hill behind the cabin with a team of horses in 1945.

Reuben scrabbled around inside the nightmare that was his refrigerator and found two brown bottles of beer. He set one by the sink and handed the other to me. I twisted off the top and extended the bottle to him, then reached past him to take the other. I wondered how long it had been since he'd been able to manage a twist top.

"Where are the dogs?" I asked. He frowned and took a long drink of the beer.

"You want to sit down?" His voice was soft and gentle, the Mexican lilt heavy.

"I can't stay that long, Reuben." I turned and looked around the room as my eyes adjusted to the dim light. "Usually the dogs are on top of me," I said.

"Someone poisoned them." He said it so simply and quietly that at first I wasn't sure that I'd heard right. But he didn't repeat himself. Instead he leaned against the sink and tipped the beer bottle. His hand, the dark brown skin tight against the bones and tendons, was steady.

"Poisoned them? When? What are you talking about?"

He waved a hand. "Three, four days. Maybe Saturday."

"That's last week," I said. "You found them dead?"

"Yes." He regarded me steadily over the beer bottle.

"Where did this happen? Right here at the house?"

Reuben shook his head. "One crawled to the truck. I find her there, half under it. The other two I find later, down in the field near the road."

"You're sure they were poisoned?"

Reuben nodded. I waited for a moment, hoping he would continue, but he remained silent.

"I wish you had called us, Reuben." He lifted one eyebrow and said nothing. After a week, the trail would be as stone cold as his dogs. "Where are the dogs now?"

"*Enterrados*." Buried. He waved vaguely in the direction of the pasture behind the trees, down toward the county road.

I took a deep breath and shook my head. "Any ideas who might have done it?"

His nod was almost imperceptible.

"Who?"

"You want another?" He indicated the beer bottle in my hand. I had yet to take a drink.

"No, thanks. Who did it, Reuben?"

He shrugged that universal Mexican shrug that meant about a thousand different things, from "I don't know" to "the world is ending tomorrow."

I tried one more time. "You know that if we can prove who did it, we can put them in jail. We can do that." I saw a trace of amusement in the old man's eyes. He didn't believe me and neither did I. We could go out to where he'd buried them, dig them up, take tissue samples, and have the lab tell us three weeks later that, sure enough, the dogs had been poisoned. But without a witness, the case would fall flat.

I changed tracks, hoping that he'd drift back to the subject of the dogs on his own.

"The ladies at the post office were a little upset this morning. Your revolver made them nervous."

"*¿Porque?*" His voice was the lightest of whispers.

"Maybe because you dropped it? They said you did." He nodded and said nothing. I mentally sent out a distress call to Estelle Reyes-Guzman. English was as awkward for Reuben as Mexican was for me. Our conversation was never going to slip into that easy gait where men speak their hearts. "Would you do me a favor and not wear it into public buildings, Reuben? Maybe even leave it at home? *¿A casa?*"

He shrugged again and set his beer bottle down near the sink. I did the same. "If you need anything, will you call me?" I realized how stupid that sounded the instant I said it, but Reuben Fuentes had the good grace not to say, "I would call you, *Señor*, if I had a telephone."

I stepped toward the doorway. The sunlight was harsh after the cool shadows of the house. "Can I stop by every couple days to check on you?"

He shrugged. "*Si quiere.*" He held onto the doorjamb as I stepped away from the cabin. "You know," he said, "it took me almost two hours to bury those dogs."

"I'm sorry," I said. "I wish you'd let me help."

"The soil is pretty hard. Lots of rocks. They could have helped, but they didn't."

"Who could have helped?"

"*Hijos.*"

"What kids?"

"On the road, you know. They were on the—" he stopped and pantomimed holding onto handlebars.

"Motorcycles? Motorbikes?"

"*Si.* The two of them. They saw me digging. They could have helped."

Reuben was living in the wrong century. If he expected two youngsters out from town on a lark to stop, hop a barbed wire fence, and offer manual labor, he was more senile than I thought... especially if they recognized him. Even saying "Good morning" to an old, smelly, gun-toting legend like Reuben Fuentes was the stuff of which Truth or Dare games were made.

"You didn't recognize them?"

He shook his head and waved a hand again.

"Do you think it was kids who killed the dogs? Maybe on a dare? Something like that?"

He shook his head immediately, reinforcing my impression that he had a culprit already in his shaky sights.

"I really wish you'd let us help you, Reuben."

"You tell Estelita to come visit," he said, and I knew our conversation was over.

I thanked him for the beer and settled into the seat of the patrol car, cussing myself for being such a gutless wonder. I should have pushed him into a chair and struggled my way through his language and mine until he understood that we could help him find the son of a bitch who killed his pets. All he had to do was tell us what he knew.

And then I realized, as I turned around and headed the patrol car out the two-track, that he understood me perfectly well. I was the one who didn't understand. Reuben Fuentes didn't want my help.

7

The lane from Reuben Fuentes's cabin to the county road was six-tenths of a mile. During the long minutes it took me to negotiate that distance without ripping out the oil pan of 310, my county car, I tried to formulate a short list of people who might have killed the old man's dogs.

Reuben's only neighbor, Herb Torrance, lived in the ranch headquarters four miles down the county road. His cattle roamed the countryside, maybe even grazed on property leased from Reuben. I didn't know for sure. But all three of the little dogs banded together wouldn't amount to much more than a fly strike on Herb's Brangus cattle.

I ruled out a casual passerby as the culprit, and that conclusion didn't require much brilliance.

Few people cruised this end of the county except during hunting seasons, and no seasons were open now. More probable, local kids might have been responsible for the killing of the dogs. To hear Glenn Archer talk, such behavior wasn't beyond his tribe.

More than once during the past year our department had gotten wind of teenagers doing stupid things under the guise of whatever dare game was the latest fad. Rumor had it that old Reuben would shoot trespassers. I had no doubt that some teenager would dare a friend to sneak as close to the old cabin as he could...and maybe even poison one of the dogs as a lark. Or all of them.

Nothing was easier than soaking a frankfurter in sweet antifreeze as a lethal tidbit. And really enterprising delinquents could cook up far worse in a chemistry class. If that had been the case, I hoped the little bastards were really clever, using a chemical that would nail their hides to the barn when the medical examiner finished his analysis.

I reached the main county road, stopping the patrol car short of the cattle guard when I saw the plume of rich, red dust being kicked up by an approaching vehicle. I waited with my windows rolled up for the car to go by, but it slowed to a crawl, the rooster-tail of dust subsiding. It was a new model Chevy Suburban, chrome running boards and all, its shiny waxed finish now layered with red dust.

As Stuart Torkelson drove the Suburban beyond the intersection with Reuben Fuentes's driveway, he grinned at me and pulled to a stop along the shoulder. Three other people were with him and they all craned their necks toward me as if I were a circus curiosity. I buzzed my window down as he got out of the Suburban and approached.

Torkelson was a huge man, beefy and florid. He played Santa Claus every year for the Lions' Club and I think he believed in his role more than the kids did.

"Now, Bill, this is one hell of a spot to run radar," he said. He leaned one huge forearm on the windowsill of the patrol car, bending down to squint inside. "What's going on?"

"Just roaming." I took his proffered hand and shook, instantly regretting it. His grip could have crushed rocks. "You touring some customers through the snakeweed?"

He turned and glanced back at the Suburban. "Yeah. A family from Austin. They're lookin' for something out of the way. A retirement spot."

"They found it."

He shot a look at me to see if I was joking, then his brow furrowed and he turned serious. "What's this I hear about Annie Hocking, not that it's any of my business?"

"She died last night."

"Well, that's what I heard, but they was saying that there was every cop car in Posadas around her place last night and this morning, early."

"Yeah, well...you know how it is. Whenever there's an unattended death, we got to follow all the procedures."

"She just keeled over, eh?"

"Looks that way."

"She sure hadn't been out and around much in past months. She called me once, back along about Labor Day, wondering what she could get for her little place. She said she was thinking of moving out with her son, somewhere out in California, I think it was." He straightened up, stretching his back. "She never did pursue it, though. Hell of a note."

"I'm sure the son will be getting in touch with you now," I said, and Torkelson shrugged as if another listing that no one would ever buy was just what he needed.

Torkelson frowned and looked off in the direction of Fuentes's property. "You been up to see the Mad Mexican this morning?" I nodded. "You know—" the realtor began, then he looked at me askance, jutting out his lower lip. "You got just a minute?"

"Sure." I knew that bending his six feet four inches down to look into my car window was hard work on a hot, sunny winter day. He stepped back when I opened the door and climbed out. We leaned against the front fender like two old friends who had the day to waste. Torkelson folded his arms across his wide chest and pointed down the county road with his chin, like a Navajo.

"I run across him last weekend, down the way just a bit."

"Oh?"

"You see where there's that outcrop of rock that comes out right to the road? And then there's that big grove of oak and piñon trees?" He pointed off to the west. I squinted and pretended I did. "Well, I own that land, worthless as it is. One day a few weeks ago I got to figuring that if I could pry the old man loose of that big pasture just on this side of that...why, that'd be a pretty good piece to develop. It'd make mine worth something, don't you see."

I didn't see, but then again I was no realtor. I didn't understand the magic of a few acres of scrub pasture. None of it was worth fifty cents to me.

"And so—" I prompted, feeling a bead of sweat accumulate on my forehead and head toward the bridge of my nose.

"Well, I got to wondering just how big that pasture was, and so last Sunday I was out here doing a little scouting, knowing that I'd be bringing these folks out sooner or later." He nodded at the Suburban. "I took me my long tape and was running some measurements on his field there." He held up a hand as if I were about to interrupt him.

"Now I know what you're going to say. No, I didn't ask him first, and I should have. I know that. But I just figured, well, hell. He won't even know, so what's the difference." He took off his sunglasses and wiped his forehead. His eyes were brilliant blue, with deep laugh lines crow-footing the corners.

"And he did mind, is that it?"

Torkelson nodded. "I hadn't finished runnin' the tape two hundred yards away from the road when there's his old Jeep, pullin' up to a stop behind my truck. Now I figured I'd just trot on down and have a chat with the old man. He got out and walked as far as the fence and when he saw that I was headed his way, he just stopped and waited. I got closer and saw that he was wearin' a gun, big as life."

"He does that," I said.

"You're damn tootin' he does. So here I was, and I decided to just be real friendly, know what I mean? I mean this land he's sittin' on is going to be a gold mine someday if the federales ever grant national monument status to Martinez Tubes down the way. So I'm walkin' kind of soft, you know what I mean? I said good mornin' to him real civil. Now he knows who the hell I am. He can see the realty sign on the door of my Suburban and all. But he just looks at me out of those little beady eyes of his and tells me to get off his land."

"Did you tell him what you were up to?"

"Hell, I tried, but that's all he would say. 'Get off my land.' And I'll be honest with you, Bill. I know I was trespassing. Hell, I know I should have asked him first. But he would have said no then, too. It was just one of those spur-of-the-moment deals, you know?"

"Well, no harm done."

Torkelson laughed ruefully. "As long as I don't end up another notch on his *pistole*," he said, mangling the Mexican word as only a Texan could.

"He's harmless," I said.

"I wasn't about to argue with him, that's for sure," Torkelson said. "He had a bee in his britches about something. No hello, or *buenos dias*, or nothin'. I was surprised that he didn't have all them dogs of his with him...sic 'em on me."

"This was last Sunday, you said?"

"In the morning. About ten, eleven o'clock."

"What did you do then?" I said it like I wanted to hear the punch line of a good joke.

"Hell, Bill, I climbed over the fence, got in my truck, and left. I turned around down the road a bit, making a show of drivin' off onto *my* land to turn around, so he wouldn't have no cause to be upset." He shrugged. "And that was that."

"Huh," I said. "You didn't happen to come out here the day before that sometime, did you?"

"No. Why?"

I looked down and busied myself with a rough thumbnail for a minute. "Because," I said after the silence between us had grown uncomfortable, "someone poisoned all three of Reuben's dogs. He thinks probably last Friday night. Maybe Saturday."

"What do you mean?"

"Poisoned 'em. Fed them something. Two of 'em died right down here by the fence line somewhere. The other managed to crawl back to the cabin. Reuben says he found the dog lying dead under his Bronco last Saturday morning."

"Well, son of a bitch. Who would do a god-awful thing like that?"

"I don't know. I'd sure like to know, though."

"Does the old man have any ideas?"

"He says he does."

"Who?"

"He wouldn't tell me."

Torkelson looked first perplexed and then, when he noticed I was gazing at him, apprehensive. "Now I hope he don't think that I had anything to do with it," he said quickly. He pushed himself away from the fender of the county car. "He's a crazy old fart, and I could see him thinkin' that."

"Relax, Torker," I said. I knew that Stuart Torkelson would sell a tourist land that had less water puddled on it than on a horned toad's back—but he wouldn't sneak around at night tossing spiked dog biscuits to other people's pets. "Reuben was in town today, and according to Carla at the post office, he was wearing his gun. If he'd thought it was you who killed his dogs, you would have known it by now. He knows where your office is. And he's had a week."

"That's a cheerful thought," Torkelson said. He took a deep breath. "I'm out and around here all the time, Bill. Tell you what. If I see anything, or anybody, that looks fishy, I'll sure as hell give you call."

"I'd appreciate that."

"And say," he said, brightening, "I hear you're off to Mexico in a little bit."

I grinned. "That's the nice thing about a small town. If you ever forget what you're doing, just ask someone...they'll know." I patted Torkelson on the arm as I moved toward the door of the car. "Estelle's having the christening for her son next week. I'm the godfather."

"He'll be a mean little *hombre* then," Torkelson said with a chuckle. "Tell Estelle and that meat-cutter husband of hers that she needs to move back to town."

"I'll tell her. It won't be anything different than what she's heard from me before."

I got in the car, slamming the door against the heat and the dust. Torkelson stepped close one more time. "You know, I came real close to selling her and her husband a house over on Bustos Avenue. Real close. Damn near closed on the deal. And then she got that job up north." He threw up his hands. "Go figure."

"I hope you sell some property to these folks, Torker," I said.

He brightened. "You ever been in Martinez Tubes?"

I shook my head. "And the second half of that story is that I never intend to go. Crawling over sharp rocks and through bat shit isn't my idea of a good time."

"Hey, you'd be surprised."

"No, I wouldn't."

"You know Herm Klein from the BLM in Las Cruces?"

"No."

"Well, him and me and a couple others went in one of them tubes that's almost two thousand feet long. Year-round ice, even."

I raised an eyebrow. "Isn't Lechugilla down at Carlsbad Caverns measured in miles, Torker?"

He grinned and slapped the doorframe of my car. "You gotta start somewhere, Bill. Mark my words—when they make that tube complex a monument, *then* you ask me which land's worth money and which isn't. I'm in on the ground floor this time." He glanced over his shoulder. "If that crazy old fart don't blow my head off first."

"He won't," I said. "He's harmless." I watched Stuart Torkelson trudge back to the Suburban where the folks were probably wondering what the confab had been all about. I pulled out onto the county road and headed back toward Posadas.

In the rearview mirror I saw Torkelson gesticulating this way and that, and the heads twisting to follow his orchestration. He was probably telling his clients that they could always expect to have efficient law enforcement should they decide to relocate to the open prairie. They probably believed him.

8

As I had begun to suspect, an afternoon's investigation turned up nothing new concerning the death of Anna Hocking. My deputies found no fingerprints that belonged to anyone other than Anna or Sheriff Holman.

That was predictable, I suppose. After almost three years as sheriff, Martin Holman still didn't know how to treat a possible crime scene.

Window sills and door knobs were clean, as were light switches and broom handles. Even the clean two-quart bottle of orange juice turned only one set of prints…Anna's. That set me even more firmly on course. The elderly lady had wanted a late snack of juice and maybe toast with jam. There was no jam in the refrigerator, but lots downstairs.

There's nothing much stronger than a nighttime snack craving—and so she'd decided against all better judgment to just hobble down the stairs one more time.

Deputy Eddie Mitchell talked with the neighbors, but at the nearby trailer park, the Sloans weren't home and the Ulibarris hadn't heard a thing until all the police cars arrived.

It wasn't a neat and tidy package, but it would do until something else broke. I was satisfied. I wasn't so confident about Reuben Fuentes.

Late that Saturday afternoon I was sitting in my office with my boots off and my feet comfortably propped up on the corner of my desk. I imagined that I was smoking a cigarette—it'd been five months, seven days, four hours, and twelve minutes since I'd had my last one. I missed them, but doctors told me my heart didn't. I hooked my hands behind my head, closed my eyes, and thought.

"Sir?" The voice jarred me, and I swung my head to see who'd intruded. Deputy Bob Torrez stood there like a new recruit, file folder in hand, bags under his eyes.

"You need to go home, Roberto," I said. "There's nothing that can't wait until tomorrow or Monday."

Torrez stepped across to my desk. "I just wanted to show you this picture, sir," he said. He opened the folder and slid an eight-by-twelve glossy toward me. I swung my feet down and leaned forward. The picture was slightly fuzzy, but I could see the pattern of what appeared to be a tennis shoe print on a clean surface.

I held the picture up and frowned, moving my head a little this way and that until I had the clearest shot through my trifocals.

"Where'd you take this?"

"I was going to show you last night, but we got busy," Torrez said in his usual serious fashion. "Remember I've been checking into the breaking and entering at Wayne Farm Supply? I found this one print inside, on the floor near where they apparently entered the building."

"How'd you take this? I'm impressed."

"Sergeant Bishop showed me a trick he'd learned from Detective Reyes when she was here," Torrez answered. "We laid a flashlight down on the floor and rolled it until the beam picked up what we thought might be footprints. At that kind of an angle, it shows up everything."

"And this print showed."

"Right. This is one of two that did. When whoever broke in stepped into the shop proper, where the floor's real dirty, they didn't leave any usable traces."

"Let me guess. The second print was left on his way out, along the same route."

"Yes sir. It didn't turn out as good. Smudged." He dug another photograph out of the envelope and handed it to me. I would have been hard-pressed to tell what it represented if I hadn't been told.

"So," I said leaning back. "The kid breaks in by prying open part of the steel siding of the building. He squeezes inside, leaving a print on the polished office floor before he hits the shop. He steals about a thousand bucks' worth of tools, and then leaves. That about it?"

"That's it, sir."

"Anything interesting taken, other than the usual hand tools and such?"

"Not that Mr. Sanchez knows of. He finished up an inventory this afternoon, and I stopped by on my way here. Just hand tools, an engine hoist, and a couple of chain saws."

"An engine hoist? Isn't that kind of big to get out through a hole in the wall?"

"It was one of those kind that you hang from the ceiling joist of a garage." Torrez held his hands up to form a circle about as big as a basketball. "Like so. Couple chains hang down from it."

"So what's your next step?"

He tapped the folder. "The print shows that the sneaker wasn't too worn. The cuts are nice and sharp. So I'm guessing it was pretty new. I was going to go down to Payless tomorrow and see if I can get a match for the brand."

"What makes you think the kid, if it was a kid, bought the shoes here in town?"

Torrez shrugged. "Just a hunch, sir. I've got three or four names on my list, and none of 'em have the kind of money to drive to Cruces to shop. I'll start here at home."

"And by the way, Roberto. While you're digging around on this burglary, there's something else I want you to do." I told him about Fuentes's dogs.

"That's a new one to me, sir," he said.

"You haven't heard any new twists on the dare games at the school? That's about all that makes sense to me."

"I'll ask around," Torrez said. "Maybe Glenn Archer will know."

"Which reminds me...I'm supposed to call him. He wants to complain again about why we won't assign fifty-five deputies to each basketball game." I waved a hand in dismissal and Deputy Torrez was about to leave when I asked, "Is Miss Reporter still riding around with you?"

Torrez actually blushed. "I dropped her off at her office earlier this afternoon. I think she had enough of waiting in the car."

"I don't doubt that," I said.

"And she told me to tell you that the first installment on her series about the department is scheduled to come out in Monday's paper."

I grinned. "Along with all the grocery store ads. I can't wait. Be sure to tell Sheriff Holman if you see him." That was a dirty trick, but what the hell. Martin would spend two wakeful nights, worrying his way toward an ulcer. Sometime when he was in a good mood I'd tell him that it was payback for smudging the prints on Anna Hocking's windowsill.

9

Anna Hocking's place became a damn magnet. I had a dozen things I could have been doing that Saturday afternoon—some were even important.

I had Deputy Robert Torrez chasing what was, in all likelihood, a bunch of kids who wanted to be burglars. I had a high school principal annoyed with me for not caring a whole lot about fistfights at basketball games. I had some freak poisoning an old man's mutts. I had guns being dropped at the post office.

In short, it was a long and frustrating list on my *Things to Do Today* pad. But I didn't accomplish any of them. Instead I found myself parking on the shoulder of County Road 19, with Anna's little adobe house just ahead.

An open chamiso- and cholla-studded field separated the mobile home park from Anna's property. I got out of the car and walked across the field, cutting a big circle around the old woman's house. Earlier, deputies with eyes far sharper than mine had searched a generous perimeter around the house, including most of this field. They had turned up nothing.

I thrust my hands in my pockets and ambled along, head down and relaxed. My boots crushed the dried sage and nettles and the aroma wafted up delicate and fragrant. Mix a little pungent piñon pine smoke with it and it would have been goddamn festive. With a start I remembered that I was supposed to pick up the little *ropon* that Augustina Baca was sewing for me.

This *padrino* business was serious stuff, I was coming to realize—even though Estelle Reyes-Guzman had given me fair warning. I had made the mistake of saying that I would pay for everything that the godfather normally paid for by Mexican custom...and Estelle had grinned. She'd told me that wasn't necessary, but I was stubborn. And she grinned wider. She didn't exactly give me a list, mind you, but it was damn near that bad.

Not a bad custom—talk the old, rich *padrino* into buying the kid's first suit of clothes. That was the first step. Estelle had known Augustina Baca for years, and the old woman had agreed to sew the tiny little tunic that the kid would wear to his baptism. The corners of Mrs. Baca's eyes had crinkled up with pleasure at her assignment. Or maybe it was pleasure at knowing the price tag.

"Ah," she had said, waving tiny wrinkled hands. "The *bautizo* is so important." She clasped her hands as if in prayer...or reckoning. And then she'd explained to me in terms far beyond my patience for listening every detail of the tiny garment that would be the talk of Tres Santos—for one day. What the hell. Estelle and her kid were special to me.

There would be more hidden expenses for the *padrino*, I had no doubt. Estelle had even mentioned one custom where all the cute little *niños* of the village cornered the defenseless *padrino* and threatened his life until he tossed fistfuls of coins to them. I'd have to change a couple bucks into pennies before I headed south.

A car door slammed somewhere behind me and jerked me back to the field and the present. I realized I had walked nearly to the small arroyo and the row of Russian olives that formed the back boundary of the pasture...and I hadn't even noticed where I had stepped, let alone seen anything significant.

I glanced toward the trailer park and saw the rear end of a dust-colored sedan pulled up in front of Miriam Sloan's place. Deputy Torrez had said he hadn't been able to talk to either the woman or her boyfriend earlier.

I turned and crossed the fifty yards of scrub to the trailer court fence, took one look at the four strands of barbed wire, and grimaced. The wire was too high and tight to straddle and I was too fat and stiff to squeeze through.

With a quiet curse I turned and made my way back to the patrol car.

Miriam Sloan's trailer had seen better days a decade before. Now it was a faded, depressing shade of blue with little fake wings on the back that had been intended to make it sporty but only looked silly. Holes in the aluminum siding had been crudely patched with discarded printing press plates from the local newspaper.

Someone had started repainting the trailer at one back corner and progressed a dozen feet with the deep blue enamel before running out of either effort or paint...or both. Even that paint was beginning to fade. I guessed the dark blue was the same vintage as the whopper-jawed porch that jutted out from the doorway and then angled down four or five steps to the gravel of the parking lot.

At least the place was neat and orderly. I figured Miriam Sloan to be on the welfare dole, and that monthly check wouldn't cover much in the way of home maintenance.

I parked behind the tan Oldsmobile and by habit jotted down the plate number on my log. One of our part-timers, a college kid, was sitting dispatch, and chasing plate numbers on the computer was good practice for him. By the time I hung up the mike, the door of the trailer was open and Miriam Sloan was standing on the top step, one hand on her hip and one eyebrow cocked heavenward.

"Afternoon, Mrs. Sloan," I said, stepping between 310 and the Oldsmobile. She didn't say anything until I reached the first shaky step of the wooden porch.

"To what do I owe this pleasure?" she asked. Her voice was low and husky. I guess there was good enough reason for her calm sarcasm. One officer or another from our department had paid her a dozen visits over the past six years, thanks to the escapades of her son, Todd.

We had extended the kid every chance too many times—maybe that was part of the problem. Still, the state pen wasn't the place for most fifteen-year-olds. Miriam Sloan could have been just a little bit grateful.

"I hope we haven't been too much of a nuisance around here the last day or so," I said. I tried for my most engaging public servant's expression.

Miriam Sloan looked puzzled. "I just now got home." She stepped forward and turned to look up the driveway toward the Ulibarris' trailer and the expanse of weeds that blanketed the rest of the mobile home park. "What happened?"

"No, it wasn't anything here, Mrs. Sloan. Mrs. Hocking died last night." I gestured to the east. "Over across the way, there."

She frowned. "For heaven's sake. How?"

"She fell, apparently. In her basement."

"Umm," Mrs. Sloan said and grimaced. It was as good a comment as any. She stepped back away from the edge of the porch and the decking creaked under her weight. At one time, she had been an attractive woman. But living on the edge had taken its toll. Too many macaroni meals had swelled her figure and the print house dress she wore stretched its buttons. Her short hair was due for another dye job, the dark roots giving her a two-tone look.

"We wanted to ask if you or Kenny happened to see or hear anything last night." I already knew the answer to at least half of my question. Kenny Trujillo had blown most of his brain cells on one chemical or another during his twenty-two years. He worked on and off at Coley Florek's wrecking yard a mile south of the interstate on Butler Avenue. Coley was bright enough to make sure that Kenny never drove the wrecker, but I guess the kid was of some value around the junkyard, stripping door handles and other useful parts off of the battered hulks that were dragged in. He didn't make enough money to threaten Miriam's welfare, even if she declared him as official family.

"I just now got home," Miriam Sloan said. "I spent two days with my sister in Albuquerque." She frowned. "But I certainly wouldn't have heard anything from way over here—even if she cried out."

"I'm sure not," I said and started to say something else when Mrs. Sloan interrupted.

"I've tried to check on Mrs. Hocking once or twice a week recently. She's been terribly frail. I was always afraid she'd fall and break a hip or something like that and end up lying there on the floor, all helpless."

I nodded. "I don't think she suffered long."

Mrs. Sloan grimaced again. "What happened? I mean, what did she do?"

"Tripped and fell down the stairs leading to the basement. That's where I found her yesterday."

"And she broke—"

"Her neck."

"Oh, my," Miriam Sloan said. "Well, Thursday night my sister called. Her husband's been so sick." She held up her hands. "She needed company so I drove on up." She looked over at her car. "I had visions of being stranded in this old wreck. I could just picture me in a ditch somewhere, half way between Quemado and who knows where else. But I made it."

"Long drive," I said. "I hope everything is going to be all right." She gave a little noncommittal shrug as if to say that she was used to handling each curve ball as it came. "What about Kenny? Do you think that he—"

"I just now walked in the door," Miriam said, trying hard not to sound testy. "I won't see Kenny until tonight." She didn't offer to ask him for me. We both knew it would be a waste of breath.

"Was Todd home, or did he go up with you?"

"Todd went to live with his father. He hasn't been staying with me."

I knew that Wilson Sloan had split the sheets half a dozen years before and the trace of venom in the way Miriam had said the word *father* told me the rift hadn't mended.

"I didn't know that," I said. I immediately wondered which one of Todd's worthless friends owned the tennis shoe that Deputy Torrez had printed, if not Todd himself. "When did he move?" I tried to sound as if I wasn't altogether overjoyed.

Miriam Sloan waved a hand and started back through the door of her trailer. "A couple of weeks ago." She smiled as if she knew a secret. "It won't work, either. He'll be back." She glanced heavenward. "Like the flu."

"You never know," I said. "Where are they at?"

"Orlando…and more power to 'em. They deserve each other."

I didn't want into the middle of that one, so I just tipped a finger to the brim of my Stetson. "Well, the Hocking place is standing empty now until her son in California finds time to straighten out her affairs. I'd appreciate it if you'd kinda look over that way once in a while. If you see anyone nosing around where they shouldn't be, I'd appreciate a call." I started to fumble out one of my cards.

"I know the number," she said acidly. "By heart."

I left the Paradise View Trailer Park nagged by one of those little groundless fears that nevertheless wouldn't go away. I wondered if, in fifteen years, Estelle Reyes-Guzman and her son would have to suffer the same kind of rift that separated Miriam and Todd Sloan.

10

By late Saturday night, I'd avoided even a catnap for the better part of thirty-six hours, and even for an old insomniac like me, that was pushing the limit. I parked 310 in the driveway of my house and went inside, welcomed by the dark, friendly silence of the old place.

With the holiday season, I had considered running a string of small Christmas lights around the recessed portal and maybe looping a strand or two over the *vigas* that faced the lane. A line of *luminarias* along each side of the driveway would have looked inviting and cheery as well, but I wasn't in the mood. Make the place look too inviting and I'd end up having company.

I closed the heavily carved front door behind me, knowing that I'd end up not doing any decorating until after Christmas… and then it'd be too late anyway. What the hell.

What I really wanted was twelve hours of uninterrupted sleep. That was wishful thinking. I knew exactly what would happen if I stretched out on the bed. The initial bliss as the bones and muscles melted into jelly and the soft aroma of the bedding and the faint mustiness of the house as they blended into a cozy potpourri would be narcotic…for about ten minutes. Then I'd start tossing and turning like an old washing machine out of balance on the agitation cycle.

I walked to the kitchen and put on a fresh pot of coffee. While the brew oozed through the calcium-choked mechanism, I considered telephoning Estelle Reyes-Guzman in Tres Santos.

Her mother didn't have a phone in her modest little adobe house, but the Diaz family just down the lane from Mrs. Reyes did. If my call managed to be patched through on the vague Mexican system, one of the myriad Diaz kids would sprint a message the hundred yards to the *Casa Reyes.*

There was no point in bothering them with a call at this hour of the night. Estelle couldn't do anything about her great-uncle's dogs anyway. The old man would survive. He'd have the distraction of a visit to Tres Santos in a week, see all his relatives, then dive back into the privacy of his shack, maybe with a truckload of new Mexican puppies to raise.

I poured myself a cup of coffee and settled into the big leather chair in the living room. I wanted a cigarette more than sleep. There were none stashed in the house and I was too tired to go after a pack. I could almost hear my eldest daughter chastising me for even thinking about smoking. I loved my children, but sometimes they ganged up on their old man.

The Christmas before, one of my sons had decided I needed a VCR and a library of videos. He'd started by sending me a copy of *The Shootist* with John Wayne and Jimmy Stewart, figuring that a movie with my two favorite stars would start me off. I sensed the fine hand of my eldest daughter, Camille, in the title choice.

My video library hadn't grown. That one video, lonely and forlorn, sat on the shelf.

Knowing that the results were guaranteed, I got up, switched on the set, and popped the tape in the machine. I'd watched the first part of the movie dozens of times—my record was reaching the point where Jimmy Stewart tells the Duke that the old gunfighter had himself "a cancer." This time, I was asleep long before that.

I awoke with a start. The television screen was a nice blank blue. The VCR had cycled into patient "wait" mode, the old gunman in the movie blown to hell and gone long before. My coffee was stone cold and I had no idea how many times the telephone had jangled. With a grunt I reached the phone and jerked it off the cradle so hard the base slid off the kitchen counter and crashed to the floor.

"Yep," I said.

"Sir, this is Gayle Sedillos." My dispatcher's voice was about as nice as any can be on a wake-up call.

"Yep. What the hell time is it?"

"Ten thirty-three, sir." I squinted at my watch and took her word for it.

"What's up, Gayle?" I was fully awake. Gayle possessed uncommonly good sense. She was worth five times what we paid her, and if she called me at home the message couldn't wait.

"Sir, Deputy Encinos just radioed in a possible homicide on County Road twenty-seven just beyond the second cattle guard off the state highway."

"A what?"

"A homicide, sir."

"I know what you said. Who, I meant."

"Deputy Encinos didn't say, sir."

"All right. I'll be there in a couple minutes. And Gayle—"

"Sir?"

"Is anyone with Encinos?"

"Deputy Abeyta," Gayle said. "He wanted to work a weekend four-to-midnight, and you left standing orders that he couldn't work that shift alone."

"Okay. Good." I heard a voice in the background and then Gayle came back on the line, this time a little more tentative.

"Sir, can you stop by and pick up a passenger on your way out?"

"A passenger?" Sheriff Holman didn't get any kick out of riding in a police car—he avoided the opportunity whenever it presented itself. I couldn't think of anyone else.

"Yes, sir. Linda Rael is here." I groaned. The young reporter kept worse hours than I did. But company wasn't what I had in mind. I started to refuse, then frowned. What the hell.

"Tell her to be standing out on the sidewalk at the corner of Bustos and Third. I won't slow down much."

I didn't bother giving Gayle any other instructions. She knew full well what to do and would make her calls to the coroner, ambulance, and Sheriff Holman in due course. Deputy Encinos would keep the crime scene intact, with the rookie Tony Abeyta to assist.

I headed out the door to 310, my pulse hammering. The second cattle guard on County Road 27 was the one by Reuben Fuentes's two-track. It didn't take much imagination to picture a confrontation out there. All that was left was to find out who'd been killed.

11

The headlights of 310 picked up Linda Rael's slight figure on the corner. The wind tugged at her long coat and her wide-brimmed slouch hat was pulled tightly down on her head. I could see the heavy camera bag slung over her right shoulder. I braked hard and she yanked open the passenger side door and was inside in one graceful, lithe movement. If I'd tried that, I would have ended up in traction for months.

As I accelerated the patrol car away from the curb I snapped on the red lights, and the pulsing beam bounced off the drab buildings as we headed out Bustos Avenue. Holiday cheer.

Clear of town, I nudged 310 a little faster. Traffic was light on the state highway and we flashed along for the first mile or so with Linda remaining silent. Her hands were tightly clasped together in her lap.

"Gayle said this was a homicide?" she asked finally.

"Apparently. Put on your seat belt. And what are you doing out at this hour?" Feeling paternal was a luxury I figured I could afford, even if her response was that it was none of my business.

"Just working...and there's a deputy already out there?"

"Yes. Paul Encino and Tony Abeyta, both."

In the dim light of the car, my peripheral vision caught the faint movement of her nod. We hurled past two big RVs driven no doubt by snowbirds trundling west. I wondered what *they* were doing out so late. When 310 was back in the proper lane, Linda turned slightly toward me. "May I ask you something?"

"Sure."

"If the body is already dead, and there's an officer already out there, why are we in such a hurry?"

I glanced over at her, amused. She was resting her right hand on the dashboard as if that might stop her from going ballistic if we crashed into something solid.

"Are you serious?" I asked.

"Yes."

I thought for a moment, trying to frame an appropriate answer, knowing that whatever I said would probably end up as a quotation in the damn newspaper. She didn't have her pencil out, though, so maybe I was safe. And I didn't slow down.

"If it's a homicide, Linda, then every minute counts. Every minute that goes by in an investigation makes the trail just that much harder to follow."

"But isn't there a working deputy already on the scene?"

I braked hard and turned off on County Road 27. The rear end of the patrol car fishtailed on the gravel and Linda transferred her grip from the dash to the door's courtesy handle.

"Yes. But he won't investigate. All Paul has done is secure the scene."

"Meaning what?"

"He makes sure no one tromps around and wrecks evidence. He makes sure nothing changes...the crime scene looks exactly the way it did when he found it. That's all he does. Unless there's someone standing over the corpse with a smoking gun or a bloody wrecking bar. Then I might let the deputy make an arrest."

Linda nodded and put her hand up on the ceiling as she saw the first cattle guard approaching. We sailed across it without much of a thump and she brought her arm back down.

"And often evidence is time-related. So," and I shrugged, "if weather conditions permit and if traffic permits, then we don't let the moss grow."

We were well away from the village and any other ranches. With no moon and a growing cloud cover, the prairie was a blank, featureless black void except for the bright tunnel bored by the patrol car's headlights. We rounded a sweeping curve whose radius gradually tightened until we were down to twenty miles an hour—and that seemed too fast as juniper limbs almost brushed the fenders. Up ahead the wink of Encinos's flashers was our beacon.

As we approached I could see a second vehicle on the shoulder of the road, far enough over that its wheels were nearly in the bar ditch. I didn't have to see the magnetic sign on the door panel to know who owned the Suburban.

Deputy Paul Encinos stood by the front fender of his county Ramcharger, waiting. The dome light was on and I could see Tony Abeyta inside. Encinos raised his flashlight in salute as I pulled up behind his four-by-four.

"Should I stay in the car?" Linda asked.

"Yes," I said and turned off the red lights.

The northwest wind had a bite as I stepped out of the car and I remembered the cloud banks I had seen earlier in the day, building in the west over San Cristobal mesa. I snapped my Eisenhower jacket closed and tucked my flashlight under my arm.

"What's up?"

Paul Encinos pointed across the road with his flashlight. If I tried hard, I might make myself believe that I could see the body. But it was just a dark lump that could as easily have been bunch grass. "Tony and I were going to drive out this way as far as the Triple Bar T gate. I saw your orders on the bulletin board to close-patrol this stretch. And there he was."

"How'd you happen to see him?"

"I had the spotlight on and was swinging it back and forth across the pasture there, trying to see dogs running or whatever."

"Good man. Then you jumped the fence and walked over?"

Encinos shook his head. "No, sir. I used the binoculars and I could see that the victim was dead."

I held out my hand and Encinos gave me the field glasses. He aimed the spotlight from the car until the corpse was centered in the pool of light. After a minute fussing with the adjustment I could make out that the body was lying roughly parallel to the roadway. The binoculars shortened the distance enough that I could see what was left of the man's face. Unless there was a grass clump in the way, even my old eyes could tell that the man's skull was missing from the bridge of his nose up.

"And you didn't climb the fence?"

"No, sir. I didn't want to mess anything up. Nobody's been over there since we arrived."

I nodded and handed the binoculars back. "Cut the top two strands of the fence," I said, pointing directly across the road. "Watch where you step."

Where the roadside fence ran along the ditch, the ground was tough bunchgrass and soil that was not much more than the bald top of an ancient limestone outcrop. A jackhammer wouldn't have left many prints. I scanned the roadway carefully while Encinos rummaged in the trunk of his car for wire cutters.

"Just let it snap back," I said when it looked like the two deputies were going to try and coil the wire after the cut. The remaining two strands were low enough that even I could hoist my bulk over without difficulty. "Walk the fence line along the road and along the two-track," I said, pointing at the road to Reuben's shack. "See where entry was made if you can."

I walked a direct, careful line to the corpse, concentrating on the ground at my feet. Nothing marred the crumpled limestone. What dry grass blades had not been mowed down by cattle or deer stood pale and unbroken in the glare of the flashlight.

The corpse was lying on its side. Brown boots, blue jeans, lightweight down jacket over a brown cotton work shirt. Stuart Torkelson hadn't changed his clothes since we'd talked earlier, not fifty yards from this spot. His head was a mess, with most of the forward vault of the skull missing.

I knelt down on one knee. There was a small puddle of blood under Torkelson's head and another near his belt buckle. I frowned. If the realtor had dropped where he'd been shot, he'd be lying in an ocean of blood, bone, and brain tissue.

I swept the light in a circle, gradually working the beam out from the corpse. Stuart Torkelson had weighed 260 if he'd weighed an ounce. If he'd been shot first and then dragged, some marks would show, however faint. I stood up.

Encinos's and Abeyta's lights had stopped at a point about twenty feet up the two-track from the cattle guard. In the distance I could hear a siren and knew that the ambulance and coroner were only moments away. "What did you find?" I called.

"I think where they crossed over," Encinos's quiet voice replied. "Come look." I retraced my steps, hopped the wire and walked around the corner of the fence to where the two deputies waited.

"The top wire is loose," Deputy Abeyta said.

"That could have been that way for days…months," I replied.

"I don't think so," Paul Encinos said. "The staple is right here." He held the flashlight close to the ground. "It hasn't been out of the wood very long. See the ends? They're not rusted like the part that was exposed."

He raised the light and held it three inches from the staple that secured the second wire. "And see? If you look real close you can see bright metal on the crown of this one, where it was pounded back in."

I straightened up with an audible cracking of joints. "Maybe. Maybe not. There might be fifty explanations for that."

"Yes, sir," Encinos said. My skepticism hadn't convinced him.

"If Torkelson was shot out here somewhere, we'll find blood, bone, and bits of brain tissue. Somewhere. If the place is clean, then he was shot somewhere else, brought here and dumped. But I don't believe that."

"Why not, sir?"

"Because it would be too much of a coincidence. The last place I saw him alive was right here, and he told me about an earlier confrontation of sorts. If he had enemies in town who killed him there, why would they choose this spot as a dumping ground? It doesn't make sense." I turned as first the ambulance and then another sedan rounded the corner and pulled to a jarring halt behind my car.

"Tony, go tell them to stay put for a while. We'll call 'em when we're ready." The officer trotted off and I turned to Encinos. "We'll take a set of photos of the body and the area tonight. Especially these staples. Use the close-up attachment. You up to that?"

"Yes, sir."

"Fine. And I want sequence and grid photos. Start at the roadway and work your way in to the body. Then document the area around the body about five feet at a time as far out as you've got film. We might not be able to see a damn thing, but at least we'll have some backup in case this weather brews some snow or rain. As soon as you've done that, let me know."

I started back toward the vehicles, then stopped. "Are your keys in the Dodge?"

"Yes, sir."

"I need to borrow it for a few minutes." I wasn't about to crash and jar my way up the two-track and across two arroyos in the Ford sedan at night. That was one reason. The other was that I could leave Linda Rael, her notebook, and her camera parked in harmless ignorance while I went to visit Reuben Fuentes.

12

Dark closed in around the little cabin like a tight envelope. With no moon and obscured stars, the pockets under the piñons and junipers sank into absolute black. The lights from the Dodge were brilliant and harsh, cutting across the junk, the old bus, and the Ford Bronco. I parked and switched off the headlights. Without them, I couldn't see Reuben Fuentes's little cabin twenty feet beyond the front bumper.

Gradually my eyes became accustomed to the ink, and I could make out a glow drifting out of the single high window on the west wall. It was the window over the sink, and the wash of light was so faint that it was like looking at a star that shows up best when caught in the peripheral vision.

I opened the door of the Dodge, grimacing against the bright dome light. As I stepped out, I saw the slight figure backlighted in the now open doorway of the cabin.

"*Buenas noches, Don Reuben,*" I said and shut the truck door. I cradled my flashlight under my arm without turning it on.

"Come inside," he said. He turned and vanished into the shadows. I felt a wave of relief that Reuben was all right, untouched by what had happened down at the road.

I stepped through the doorway and saw a single lamp across the room in the corner by the fireplace. The bulb couldn't have been more than ten watts, the light further muffled by a dark brown shade that had once been burlap before the moths and spiders got to it. A book lay in the chair.

"I'm sorry to disturb you so late, Reuben," I said, pushing the door closed behind me.

"You want a beer?" He shuffled toward the refrigerator and I quickly held up a hand.

"No, really. Thanks just the same." My refusal had no effect. He opened the small door and brought out first one brown bottle and then another. He set one by the sink and frowned.

"I don't know where the opener is," he said almost in a whisper. He rummaged through the detritus around the sink.

"It's a twist-off," I said. I reached over and opened one of the bottles, then handed it to him. I left the other on the counter, unopened.

"*Siéntese,*" he said, indicating one of the two straight chairs. I chose the one without the cat.

"How have you been?" I asked.

"Since this morning? *Bien.*" He picked up the book that had been in his chair and sat down. "You have news of *Estelita.*"

"No. That's next weekend, Reuben." I leaned forward, rested my forearms on my knees, and folded my hands. There was no fire in the fireplace, but the cabin was snug and warm. "We've got us a problem down by the road."

For a minute I thought he'd forgotten my presence and had started reading again. But after a bit he closed the book and carefully laid it on the small lamp table next to his beer bottle. His hands composed themselves in his lap and in the dim light I couldn't tell if he was regarding me with interest or simply had his head pointed in my general direction.

"What kind of problem do you have?" Reuben asked.

"One of your neighbors got himself shot."

"*Lo siento.* It happened earlier?"

"Yes. We think so. We don't know when, for sure."

Reuben shifted a little in his chair and groped in his shirt pocket for a cigarette. He tamped both ends with care and then lit it with a kitchen match that he scratched against the stones of the fireplace. The smoke smelled too good…I damned near asked him for one myself.

"I heard two shots, *señor.* Two. I think it was two."

"When was this, Reuben?"

"As I remember it was after the sun went down. Maybe seven o'clock. Maybe later. Maybe eight. I don't remember with certainty." He smoked in silence for a while. I was sure he was thinking the story through and I didn't interrupt him. Finally he said, "I thought that it was probably hunters across the road."

"The shots sounded far away?"

"Yes."

"Did you drive down to see?"

"No."

"Did you hear or see anything else? Out of the ordinary, I mean."

He shook his head. "So tell me...who was it?"

"Stuart Torkelson, Reuben."

"*¿Verdad?*" He frowned. "Somebody beat me to it, then."

"Beat you to it?"

"You know, *señor*, that he and I have our arguments. He thinks he should have deed to every acre on earth, this man. And then sell it to foreigners from—" he waved his hand in frustration. No doubt folks from back east were foreigners to him.

"We found him in your field, Reuben."

"What was he doing there?"

"I don't know. I was hoping you could tell me."

"*No se,*" the old man said. "If you mean the field down by the road, he was there earlier, too."

"I know. He told me this afternoon."

"I do not know why he was there."

"We'll be going over that field and the area around it pretty carefully, Reuben. We'll be down there the rest of the night and probably all day tomorrow." I stood up and stepped over to the sink. I put the bottle of beer he'd offered me back in the refrigerator.

The inside of the fridge was as dark and forbidding as the rest of the cabin. I had never won the Good Housekeeping seal of approval for my home's cleanliness either, but at least I could still recognize many of the items in my refrigerator.

I turned around, leaning against the edge of the sink. My eyes had adjusted enough that I could make out the mantel of the fireplace. A piece of what might have been lava rested there, its shiny black surface muted by cobwebs and dust. In almost the exact center of the mantel lay a large revolver.

"I came by to ask your permission, Reuben. To ask if we can search the field. We might be able to find something that will help us."

"*Claro.*"

As I spoke I made my way over to the fireplace and picked up the revolver. It was a single-action Colt, and it smelled as musty as everything else in the cabin. And it was fully loaded. I laid it back down. "If you see anything else, or hear anything, will you call me, Reuben?"

He nodded.

"Someone will be down at the cattle guard most of the night if you think of anything. Just holler." He stood up with considerable effort and followed me to the door. The old man and his rude cabin were instantly lost in the shadowless night as I turned the Ramcharger around and drove back down the lane.

The number of lights, blinking red and otherwise, had grown exponentially in the few minutes I had been gone. I parked the Dodge in the middle of Reuben's lane, nose to nose with Sheriff Martin Holman's black Buick.

I had no more than opened the door when Deputy Tony Abeyta materialized. His face was animated.

"We found where the shooting took place, sir."

"Good work. Where?"

"Just over there, this side of that grove of piñons." He aimed his flashlight and the beam stabbed across the pasture, the light lost in the sea of crisscrossed spots from three patrol units and half a dozen other flashlights.

I frowned, puzzled, and muttered, "Why did they drag him almost a hundred feet after they shot him?"

"Sir?"

"Nothing, Tony. You got the place roped off?"

"Yes, sir. And Bob is almost finished taking pictures."

Deputy Robert Torrez had climbed out of bed for this one, too. That didn't surprise me. Before dawn, most of the Posadas County Sheriff's Department employees would have trekked across this field for one reason or another. And that included the sheriff himself, Martin Holman.

I stood at the barbed wire fence, my right hand resting lightly on the top strand, as I watched Holman make his way across the rough ground toward me.

The sheriff was medium height, medium weight, his hair medium brown, medium thick, and medium long. When I'd first met him, I'd thought that he was medium stupid, too. But he wasn't, really. The used car lot he'd operated before the election made him a fair living. His brother still ran the place.

He'd won the election on one of those sweeping tides of promises for fiscal responsibility to which voters fall prey periodically. During the first months of his tenure, he'd discovered that money hadn't been wasted in the department. When we requested a new patrol unit it was because the piece of junk it replaced was just that—junk. He'd discovered that we were understaffed, undertrained, and underbudgeted in general.

And my estimation of him had soared when Martin Holman started spending his time doing what he did best—lobbying legislators for more money. He was no cop, though. I tried my best to forgive his occasional gaffes when he decided to play at being one. We'd made it through three years of his tenure with few embarrassments.

Holman reached the fence. He was breathing hard.

"Christ, Bill," he said.

I didn't know whether he was referring to the crime itself, the late hour and chilly wind, or my being absent when he arrived…or all of the above. So I said, "I was just up at Reuben's."

"Well this is a hell of a thing, Bill," Holman said. "First the Hocking woman and now this. I mean, Stuart Torkelson, for God's sake."

I nodded in the darkness.

"What the hell happened out here?" Holman asked.

"We don't know yet," I said. "Torker got himself shot. Deputy Abeyta was telling me they found the spot where the shooting happened."

"Way the hell over there by the trees," Holman said, waving a hand. "They've got the place roped off. I started to walk across and I thought Bob Torrez was going to chop my head off. Christ."

"Well, sir, you know how it is. Sometimes it's just the tiniest bit of evidence that makes a case. If someone steps in the wrong place and destroys that evidence—" I let the rest of it go. Holman had heard the same story often enough. He had heard me chew ass during previous investigations when deputies didn't pay attention to clumsy feet or hands, and most of the time he had the good sense to stay out of the way.

"Yeah, yeah," he said, his tone tinged with impatience. "So what did the old man say?"

"He heard two shots."

"That's all?"

"That's all. He said they were in the distance and that he ignored them."

"That's hard to believe."

I looked at the smudge in the darkness that was Holman. I couldn't see his face, but the sharpness of his voice surprised me. "How is it hard to believe, sir?"

"Well, come on. You know how old man Fuentes is as well as I do. Someone sneezes around his property and he's out the door, waving some damn gun in your face." He lowered his voice. "I heard about what happened at the post office earlier."

"That was a separate incident, Sheriff."

"Maybe. The old man's crazy, is what I say."

"He may be old and crazy, but he's not capable of this. He and Torkelson had their differences, I'll admit that." I pulled my coat a little tighter against the wind. "In fact, according to Stuart they had a go-around a week or so ago. But that doesn't mean—"

"What go-around?" Holman interrupted.

"They had a little set-to about property boundaries. I talked with them both. It has nothing to do with this."

"How do you know that?"

I started to answer but then hesitated. I didn't know, that was the trouble. "I just don't think so, that's all. For one thing, if Torkelson was actually shot where Deputy Abeyta says he was, then someone had to drag the body from there," and I pointed across the field toward the cluster of lights, "to there," and I indicated where Torkelson's body still lay, covered with black plastic. "That's probably a hundred feet or more."

"Anyone could do that," Holman said.

"Come on, Martin. Not anyone. Torkelson was huge. He must have weighed two-fifty at least. Reuben Fuentes couldn't move him two feet, let alone a hundred."

"Maybe after he was shot he staggered—"

"Sheriff, did you look at the body?"

"No, not yet." The hesitation in his voice was obvious. He didn't want to look.

"Then let's go do that."

13

The harsh lights added to the ghoulish scene. Sheriff Martin Holman pulled his Stetson down low over his forehead and hunched against the growing chill of the night wind. His hands were thrust in the pockets of his coat. His face was stone white and his upper lip quivered a little now and then.

If he was going to vomit, I hoped he'd have the good sense to move far away, downwind. He didn't like what he saw, and neither did I.

We pieced it together this way. Seventy-eight feet, four and one-half inches southwest of Stuart Torkelson's corpse was a single splotch of blood the size of a tea-cup saucer. It was nearly circular, puddled for the most part on a bald patch of limestone. Part of the circumference of the puddle touched a clump of dried grama grass.

With a tape measure stretched tight between that single glob of blood and the toe of Torkelson's left boot, we then measured fifty-one feet, three and three-quarter inches toward the body. At that point we taped a perpendicular line off to the north another seven feet, eight inches to the first of many blood patches there.

And at this site, it was more than a single, neat puddle. The spray of blood, bone, and tissue covered a fan-shaped area nearly sixteen feet across.

Looking as if some gruesome surveyor had been at work, a cheery red flag with its wire post pushed into the ground marked a large fragment of skull and attached tissue that had flown almost nineteen feet out from the first droplet of blood.

As the camera flashguns continued their private electric storms, Holman looked at a preliminary drawing that Deputy Torrez had handed him. I held a flashlight so he could hold down the corners of the page against the wind.

"If this is Torkelson's blood," Holman said, pointing at the solitary blood puddle, "then he was wounded first here and then maybe stumbled over to here." He pointed at the spot where the spray began.

"Yes. If that's his blood. We don't know that yet."

"How—" Holman stopped. He grimaced and shook his head, looking off into the night. When he'd collected his thoughts and fought his supper back down, he continued, "If this is where he was standing when his head was blown off, how did he finish up some twenty-seven feet away, over here? Did someone carry him? Drag him?"

"It could have happened any number of ways," I said. "He might have been running when he was shot. His momentum could have carried him that far, easily. Even if he'd just been walking away, or staggering, he could have covered that distance."

"So he wasn't necessarily dragged, then," Holman said. He snapped the notebook closed and pushed it in his pocket. "He had a confrontation with someone, maybe saw something he shouldn't have, and was shot."

"That's possible."

"The first time he maybe fell down. Maybe on his hands and knees. Enough blood pumps through his clothing that it puddles on the rock back there." Holman stopped and turned, staring over at the mass of lights that bathed the little puddle of blood. I was impressed that he'd managed to think the possibilities that far through.

"And then he pushes himself to his feet, turns, and staggers off toward his Suburban, over there." He pivoted and pointed toward the road. The Suburban was almost in a straight line with Torkelson's final line of travel. "He manages fifty feet or so before the killer catches up with him and—" He let the rest hang.

"It could have happened that way."

Holman looked at me, one eyebrow raised. "You don't think that's what happened? So what was he doing out here, in the middle of nowhere, at night, for God's sake?"

"I don't know, Martin. Right now, what you suggest is as good a theory as any we've got."

"This is the old man's land, isn't it?"

"I think so, yes. This hill here," and I gestured to the west where the piñon and oak grove rose up on the limestone swell, "is actually Torkelson's, I think."

"Well, the old man and Torkelson had an argument earlier. That's what you said. And we know Fuentes always carries a gun, and we know that he would use it. It's easy to see—"

"Now wait a minute, sheriff," I said quickly. "Reuben Fuentes did have a minor confrontation last Sunday with Torkelson, that's true. But he doesn't always carry a gun. In fact, in past months, it's been rare that he does. And the last time he shot anyone, as far as I know, was in 1920, in old Mexico."

"There are plenty of rumors to the contrary, Bill," Holman said.

"And that's just what they are...rumors. For one thing, Reuben is too frail to be any part of this."

"He's not too frail to pull a trigger."

"Martin, think about what you're looking at here. If Reuben pulled the trigger and Torkelson staggered away from him, Reuben would have had to have been quick enough to catch up with him. He's not. He hobbles, and a slow hobble at that."

"What about earlier, in the post office? He was carrying a loaded revolver then. You said so yourself."

I took a deep breath. "Yeah, he was carrying one in the post office. And, if anything, that proves my point. According to Carla Champlin, Reuben was too frail to even pick up the gun after he dropped it. He was using a cane as well. He's upset over what someone did to his dogs, but he—"

"Sir?" Deputy Paul Encinos appeared as a silhouette, backlit by the floodlights to the west. "You should come look at this."

Holman and I followed him across the pasture, staying away from the line that had been laid on the ground between the blood remains.

Encinos stopped near the first blood stain and pointed with his flashlight. "From here, we measure thirty-one feet and some inches to there." He swung his flashlight to the west until the beam touched a grove of runty, gnarled Gambel's oaks that grew from the foot of a low limestone escarpment.

"And what did you find?" Holman asked. I could hear the excitement in his voice as he recovered from his initial reaction to brains, bone, and blood.

Encinos, now joined by Tony Abeyta and Bob Torrez, made his way toward the oaks. Holman and I followed. I didn't like all those boots tramping the ground, but the deputies had done their preliminaries before calling us.

Encinos stopped and held his light. "We'll get the generator and portables over here in a minute, but you can see pretty clearly even with just the flashlights," he said.

In a spot where over the years leaves and runoff had deposited the makings for soft dirt at the base of the escarpment, the ground was disturbed by recent digging. The layer of leaves had been disturbed, too. I could see the line farther up the bank where the neat seasonal layering of the leaves had been interrupted.

When whoever it was had finished digging, they'd swept leaves back in place, trying to conceal the spot.

"So what do you suppose is there?" I asked.

Deputy Bob Torrez, methodical and careful as usual, snapped off his flashlight and slipped it in his pocket. "Do you want to wait until morning to dig it up?"

I started to reply but Sheriff Martin Holman beat me to it. "Right now," he said. "I don't think we should wait. If this is somehow connected, and if we wait until morning, then the trail will just be colder than it already is."

"Sir?" Torrez asked, looking at me.

"The sheriff is right," I said.

Torrez immediately turned to the other deputies. "We'll be a while taking the photos before we disturb anything. Tony and Paul, why don't you bring up the burro."

The burro was the small portable generator that would provide all the light we'd need to make an artificial daytime in this lonely spot.

While the deputies assembled their equipment, I made arrangements for the removal of Stuart Torkelson's remains. He'd lain out in the cold long enough.

14

I couldn't think of anything much more macabre than opening a possible grave on a starless, moonless, wind-swept December night. I gave Linda Rael a choice—the safe, warm comfort of a locked patrol car or the dark, cold, blustery pasture.

Shivering against the wind, she clutched camera bag and notebook and followed me across the field toward the spot where the burro chugged away, powering four big arc lamps. For a radius of fifty feet around what we assumed was a gravesite, the light was brighter than high noon of a cloudless June day.

"What's buried there?" she asked and I had to give her credit. There was more excitement than apprehension in her voice. Still, with fifty yards to go, she walked past me, her pace accelerating until she reached the reassuring light and the circle of armed cops.

"We don't know," I said to her back. I wasn't willing to guess.

Before disturbing the soil, we completed a grid search, thoroughly inventorying the contents of each square meter of an area a dozen times bigger than any possible grave might be.

"You think we need photos, too?" Torrez asked at one point and I nodded.

"Film's cheap."

Finally, at nearly four in the morning, with the first small pellets of moisture salting the air, we began to dig. Working like a bunch of archaeologists with badges, we removed the loose dirt a shovelful at a time, dumping the soil through a small, coarse screen. It was the same sort of screen that folks hunting Anasazi remains would use to sift out projectile points, pot shards, or bone fragments. We didn't care about the pot shards.

As the deputies worked, I realized that the young reporter was standing so close to my elbow she was almost leaning on me. Her breath pumped out in rapid exhalations and her eyes never left the spot of disturbed earth.

"Do you need a warrant to excavate someone's private property like this?" she asked at one point, and I shook my head.

"Not when the owner gives us permission."

"Do you think Mr. Fuentes had anything to do with this?"

"We don't know, Linda. Well, wait a minute. No, we don't think he did."

Before she had a chance to question that, Tony Abeyta stopped digging, the tip of the shovel in the dirt. "I hit something," he said.

Five minutes later, enough dirt had been gently removed that all of us could see the patch of brown fur.

"Looks like a dog or something," Abeyta said.

"I imagine you'll find three of them, then," I said.

Linda Rael looked up at me quickly. "You knew what was here all the time?"

The steady two-cycle bray of the generator made it hard to hear. I laid a hand on her shoulder. "Say again?"

"Did you know what was buried here?"

"Not for sure, no." I caught movement out of the corner of my eye and turned. A fair contingent of cars had assembled down on the county road, and one of our part-timers worked with two of the auxiliaries—the Sheriff's Posse they called themselves—to keep the curious from hopping the fence.

I never ceased to wonder at folks who sat at home listening to scanners, then charged out into the night when something juicy was going down. If they were lawyers I could understand it. But most of the people who drifted by, idling their cars along at a slow walk, were just out on a lark, hoping they would catch a glimpse of something truly repulsive.

I suppose we could have held up each one of the poisoned dogs as it came out of the ground. Hell, front page news photos they'd be. But Linda Rael didn't cooperate. As each one of the pathetic animals was uncovered, her camera remained bagged and her notebook remained in her coat pocket. Apparently there was a limit to what the *Register* wanted on its front pages.

The animals had been laid side by side in the grave like the good friends they'd been. Old Reuben hadn't been able to dig very deep…the hole was less than eighteen inches when we were finished.

"I'm surprised the soil's as deep as it is," Martin Holman said. I felt escorted now, with him on one side and Linda on the other.

"Kind of a collection spot for erosion off the hillside," I said, offering the extent of my geology background. "You can get pockets of soil that are six or seven feet deep in places along the bottom of these bluffs."

But Holman wasn't interested in lessons from Mr. Science.

"So why did Stuart Torkelson walk up here to this spot, and why was he shot?"

"I don't know, sheriff."

"You said the old man buried the dogs last week? I mean, is that what you said?"

"That's what he told me."

Holman fell silent as he watched the deputies finish up their photography session. The corpses of the dogs certainly weren't daisy fresh, that was for sure.

Deputy Torrez jabbed the point of his shovel into the center of the hole's bottom. "I guess that's it," he said.

"When are you going to arrest him?" Holman spoke directly into my ear. Either he didn't want to shout over the generator or he didn't want the reporter in on the conversation.

"Arrest who?" I turned so we were face to face.

"The old man. Fuentes."

"I'm not going to arrest him, Martin."

"Why not? What more evidence do you need? The body was found on his property, associated with this—" he ran out of words and waved a hand at the dead dogs and their shallow grave. "And when you figure that half the time he runs around waving a loaded gun under people's noses—"

"Martin," I said and took him by the elbow. I led him several paces away. Linda shrugged off her hood, freeing up her ears for maximum pickup. But she had the good sense not to follow us.

"In the first place, yes, the old man sometimes carries a gun. He happened to do so in the post office, and he dropped the damn thing. I don't deny that. And yes, he had a confrontation with Torkelson last weekend. But Stuart isn't—wasn't—the type to do anything to exacerbate the affair. Hell, he told me about it the minute he saw me. If there had been any other problem, he would have called us. He's got a goddamned telephone right in his Suburban, for God's sake."

Holman shook his head vehemently. "You're right there, Bill. Stuart Torkelson wouldn't do anything to pick a fight. And it looks to me like he was trying to make a beeline right back to his truck when he was shot. It's the old man who went off his rocker and nailed Torkelson before he had a chance to explain."

I rummaged in my pocket for a cigarette for a full minute before I remembered that I had probably quit smoking.

"Explain what, sheriff?"

"Well, I don't know what. But something."

"What would make Torkelson jump the fence? He knew it was Reuben's property and he knew the old man didn't want him on it. Reuben thinks Torkelson was trying to force him to sell."

"He had to see something," Holman said.

"Yes, he had to see something. What?"

The sheriff shrugged. "I still say you've got enough evidence to hold the old man for a preliminary hearing."

"For what? Where's he going to go?"

Holman looked up and almost smiled. "Mexico, Bill."

"Come on."

"I'm serious. Hell, he's got relatives down there, just what… twenty-five miles away? If he knows we're on him, I'll bet you a hundred dollars that he's gone before we can blink an eye."

"I'm not going to throw a ninety-year-old man in jail just because of this," I said. "He buried his dogs here. He's got a right to do that. The rest is just conjecture."

"He doesn't have the right to shoot one of our leading citizens who was just out minding his own business."

"Martin, think on that one, will you? Stuart Torkelson obviously *wasn't* minding his own business. If that had been the case, he'd be home in a comfortable bed right now. He wouldn't be dead. What we're going to have to find out is what he *was* doing out here. And what someone else was doing out here."

Holman took a deep breath and jammed both hands in his coat pockets. The rain was still light, but the small drops were icy cold, driven by the wind out of the west.

"So what are you going to do?"

"I'm going to talk to Reuben again. In the morning. And I'm going to call his grandniece as soon as I get back to the office. And I'm going to wait until the medical examiner has something concrete to go on before jumping to conclusions."

"What's it going to take before you figure you have enough to make an arrest?" Holman asked.

"You mean before I'll take Reuben Fuentes into custody? A whole lot, Martin. A whole lot."

He shook his head. "I think you're too close to this one, Bill. I really do." He stepped around me as if he was going to join the deputies at the hole. But he stopped, turned, and added, "If Reuben Fuentes wasn't related to Estelle Reyes-Guzman, he'd be in the lockup right now. And you know it."

Martin Holman's sudden attack of spine surprised me. But he was dead wrong on all counts. Maybe he was just playing the hard-driving sheriff for Linda Rael's benefit. That was all right, as long as he didn't get in the way, or do something stupid on his own.

I touched Linda's elbow. "I'm going back to the office. Want to come along?"

"Aren't they going to rebury the dogs?" she asked. Her voice was small and she was shivering.

"No. They'll take them for analysis. The old man didn't press the issue, but as long as we've gone this far, we might as well find out what killed 'em. You never know."

She saw the black plastic bags laid out on the ground and she turned away. "I'm ready," she said.

We were nearly back to the village limits when she asked, "What happens now?"

I shrugged. "We wait for the medical examiner's report on Torkelson's corpse and any of the other physical evidence. A couple of the deputies will be working out there all day tomorrow, double-checking that we didn't miss anything. We'll interview the old man." I shrugged again.

"Do you think he did it?"

"Don't you start, now."

She almost laughed. "Well, everyone's heard the stories about him."

I swung into the department parking lot and pulled up next to the gasoline pumps. "Linda, we can't arrest a man based on what folks say they've heard...or what they haven't heard. We'll do what the evidence tells us to do."

It was pellet snow, then, pinging off the windshield. I was loath to stand outside another minute, pumping gasoline into the county gas-guzzler. But I'd thrown enough fits in the direction of young deputies who'd put a half-empty patrol car away that I was trapped now. I shrugged my coat tighter and got out.

"Besides," I said over the top of 310 as Linda prepared to make a break for the warmth and coffee of the office. "If Reuben Fuentes was guilty of murder, he wouldn't have just sat up there in his little cabin, letting us dig the hell out of his field."

She nodded and started to walk inside. But she stopped and turned around. "Do you call in other agencies?"

"What do you mean?"

"The state police, maybe. You know, for help."

"If need be, of course. But our people are pretty good at what they do, Linda." She pulled her coat tighter against the wind and walked inside.

While I waited for the nozzle to click off, I thought about the old Mexican in his tiny shack. At first I had thought that maybe it wouldn't be a bad idea to bring him into town for the night, for his own protection. But there were some pieces that didn't fit.

Reuben Fuentes might be damn near senile, maybe half blind and almost stone deaf when he needed to be...but let someone sneeze near his land and he was out the door with pistol or rifle or shotgun in hand.

Hunters didn't roam his property during deer season without challenge...and earlier Stuart Torkelson hadn't read two numbers off his tape measure before the old man was at his backside. And now, the old man had allowed a revival-sized crowd of people to tramp one of his pastures, dig his earth, and disturb the eternal rest of his hounds. That wasn't like him.

I screwed on the gas cap, snapped the door closed, and sat back inside the car to jot all the bookkeeping gibberish in the log.

I'd committed some real boners in my twenty-three-year career in law enforcement, generally because I had assumed, with complete certainty, that I was right at the time. I knew that Reuben Fuentes hadn't shot Stuart Torkelson. My unflinching certainty was making me nervous.

15

By eight-thirty that morning, we were handed one of the missing puzzle pieces, Martin Holman issued an order, and I couldn't put off calling Estelle Reyes-Guzman any longer.

I closed my office door against interruptions and found the number I wanted on the roller file. The signals were traveling no more than thirty miles as the crow flies—probably less. But for efficiency, I might as well have been calling the moon.

Finally a small voice came on the other end.

"*¿Hola?*"

"*¿Quien es?*" I asked.

"*Tinita,*" the tiny voice said, well named.

"Tina," I said, "is your father or mother home?"

A long pause followed my sudden excursion into English. "Tina?" I repeated.

"*¿Hola?*"

I closed my eyes with frustration, trying to remember back forty-seven years to when I was a high school junior and Mrs. Hempsted had tried to twist my hopelessly Scotch-Irish tongue around Spanish I.

"*Hija, quiero hablar* with…*con* your *madre* or *padre.*"

That brought a response. The kid probably thought she was talking to a drunk. "*Un momento,*" she said primly. A couple loud clanks as the phone was dropped on the table were followed by a bellow of startling proportions from such young lungs.

"Hello?" a teenage voice said after a minute. "Who's calling, please?"

I knew that Felicia Diaz was fourteen, and that sounded about right for this voice.

"Is this Felicia?"

"Yes."

"Oh, good. Felicia, this is Undersheriff Bill Gastner up in Posadas."

"Good morning, sir."

She was so damn polite I wanted to bottle her manners and sell them to parents of American teenagers.

"How's your family enjoying the holidays?"

"Fine, sir. Even Roberto is home for a week." Roberto Diaz was twenty-two or so and studying to be a dentist. Where he found the money for that was a mystery to me. I heard a voice in the background and Felicia said, "One moment, please." She did a good job of covering the speaker of the phone, but I managed to hear her say something that included *policia* in it.

"Sir, here is my father."

"Thanks, Felicia. You have a good holiday. See you next week at the christening."

Roman Diaz's voice was hearty and heavily accented. "Señor Gastner. Good to hear from you!"

"The same, Don Roman. How's the family?"

"Fine, sir. Fine. When are you coming down? And let me assume that you need to reach Estellita?"

"You read my mind. I sure do. Is there any way you could send someone down the lane?"

"Tinita is on the way," he said. "Do you want me to have Estelle call you or—"

"I'll hold on if I might." I had a good connection and didn't want to risk losing it. Roman Diaz and I exchanged pleasantries about the weather, family, and the upcoming christening of Estelle's infant son.

In no more than five minutes, our conversation was interrupted by a shout from Tinita's tiny lungs. When Estelle came on the line she was breathing hard.

"Make yourself comfortable, doll. We're going to be talking a while. This is Gastner."

"Now what have you done?" She said it as a joke, in between breaths. "Are you in Posadas?"

"Of course. Where did you think I'd be?"

She laughed. "No way of telling, sir." She took a deep breath. "How are you?"

"Fine. I really am. We've got a little problem of a different sort up here."

"Oh? *Que?*" Her voice, once she found her breath, was rich and velvety.

"You remember Stuart Torkelson?" When she didn't respond immediately I added, "He's a realtor here…has been for years."

"I know the name. I'm not sure I ever met him…wait. A great big man? White hair like one of those people in the silver hair commercials?"

"That's him."

"Right. He tried to sell Francis and me a home once. And I saw him again at a Lions Club luncheon where I was the guest speaker. He introduced me. What did he do?"

"He got himself killed."

"I'm sorry to hear that. How?"

I hesitated. "Someone shot him."

"Right there in town?"

"No. About seven miles southwest of the village."

She didn't miss a beat. "Out by Uncle Reuben's place?"

"Yes. One of the deputies was close-patrolling the area after an earlier complaint we had, and he found the body. About fifty feet off the road in that big pasture that fronts on both the county road and the old man's two-track."

"And he'd been shot?"

"Yes. Twice." I told her every detail of what we'd found, including Torkelson's tale of his confrontation with Reuben earlier.

"I don't think so, sir," she said when I'd finished.

"Neither do I. But it's harder to argue with Martin Holman when he's got the medical examiner behind him."

"What do you mean?"

"Well, earlier I was operating under the assumption that a shotgun was used for the head wound. We didn't move the body, and we didn't do much of an on-site examination. The weather wasn't cooperating, it was dark—that sort of thing. We took a half million photos and figured the examiner would tell us all we needed to know."

"Sure. The deputies did a grid search for shell casings and the like?"

"Yes. And found nothing. But that's not the point. The belly wound was caused by a heavy-caliber handgun, fired from far enough away that there was no flash burn, no powder. The slug hit him just above the belt and drove right on through. Through and through."

"So no recovered slug."

"That's right. But Estelle, this is where I went wrong, I guess. The head wound was pretty massive. Lots of skull case missing, that sort of thing. I saw the wound and assumed shotgun, held close."

"I don't think Reuben ever owned a shotgun in his life."

"That's what I was figuring. But the medical examiner says the head wound was caused by a handgun, probably the same caliber as the other wound...and the damn thing was held so close that the corona was only a couple inches in diameter."

"Under the chin?"

"Almost. The point of entry was right on the left jawbone, just in front of where the bone starts to curve upward toward the ear. The M.E. says the bullet hit that heavy bone and mushroomed right away."

"Huh," Estelle said. "And let me guess the bad news. Uncle Reuben was carrying one of his guns when he and Torkelson had their set-to a week ago?"

"That's what Torkelson told me."

"And he was wearing it in the post office too?"

"Yes. Three witnesses. No doubt about it."

There was a long moment of silence and then Estelle said, "It doesn't look good, sir."

"Nope."

"You find a corpse shot to death on the property of a person who you know carries a gun and who has been known to use it in the past and you're bound to make certain conclusions."

"Yep."

"And Sheriff Holman wants you to arrest Reuben?"

"At least hold him for a preliminary hearing."

"I suppose I can't blame him. But he doesn't know Reuben Fuentes like I do...or like you do."

"No, he doesn't. But he's the sheriff. And he's got the district attorney's ear. They sit at the same table during Rotary." Estelle ignored the acid in my tone.

"You can't talk him out of it? I mean, where does the sheriff think Reuben will go?"

"He thinks the old man will run to Mexico."

"*Por Dios*," Estelle said with considerable acid of her own. "*Ahora el se las da de experto.*"

"Speak English, dammit."

"Sorry, sir. I said now he wants to be the expert. Why can't he stick to talking with the legislature about the budget?"

"Come on, Estelle. He's not as much of an idiot as we first thought, three years ago."

"He is if he thinks Reuben would leave his place for Mexico."

"There's always a chance."

"No, there isn't. He's so old and…and…*caduco* that he probably doesn't remember what direction the border is."

I let that pass and said, "Sheriff Holman wants to go out this morning and bring him in for questioning."

This time, there was more than exasperation in Estelle's voice. "This is going to kill him, sir. If he thinks for one minute that he's going to jail for something…especially something he didn't do, it'll kill him."

"Yes."

"Should I come up?"

"Yes."

"I can be there in an hour. Will you have Holman at least wait until I get there?"

"It's a promise, Estelle."

16

Holman returned to the office a few minutes later, after I told our dispatcher to bring him in. Hell, he'd been out tramping around that field long enough. I didn't want him dreaming up any more complications. He stood in the doorway of my office, his hands in his coat pockets, Stetson pulled low over his forehead like a real goddamned lawman.

"I don't think you're right in this," he said, sounding like some goddamned counselor.

"Yes, I am," I said. I was blunt, but sometimes that was the only kind of instrument that worked on Holman.

"And if we wait to arrest the old man, what are you planning?"

"Look," I said, exasperated. A fleeting memory surfaced of a former sheriff, Eduardo Salcido. Salcido had had the good sense to hire me, twenty-three years before. I'd learned his habit of telling people things once and letting it go at that. Martin Holman liked to hear the same song half a dozen times, maybe hoping that the words would change.

I moved my empty coffee cup two inches to the right, as if it were in my way. "Look, sheriff. We've got a uniformed deputy parked at the entrance to Reuben's property, with the county road sealed off beginning at the intersection with the state highway." I held up my hands. "As far as I'm concerned, that's a waste. I mean, the damn road was open all night, when we were measuring and popping flashbulbs. Nobody's going out there. Nobody's going to touch anything. And most important, Reuben Fuentes isn't going to slip out from under our noses and slide into Mexico."

"I don't see why you have to have Estelle Reyes-Guzman on hand before you do anything. She doesn't work for us."

"I know that." I paused to take a deep breath, my patience running thin. "Reuben Fuentes speaks English about as well as you and I talk Spanish. I need someone he trusts to talk with him. Estelle is nearby, and obviously he trusts her. It just makes sense. I want him to understand what's happening to him."

Holman nodded slightly and straightened his Stetson. "I was thinking of signing up for beginning Spanish at the community college this spring."

I stared at him for a moment in disbelief. I didn't know what to say, but Holman saved me the trouble.

"So...the minute Reyes-Guzman arrives, we go out," the sheriff said.

"You're not planning a cavalcade, I hope?"

"What do you mean?"

"I mean," I said, "that just Estelle and I go out and bring the old man in. That's more than enough. Anything beyond that is just plain silly."

Holman eyed me askance, his eyes carrying that practiced hard glint that television actors adopt when they're playing the crusty lawman. "You know, it is possible that the old man did it," he said quietly. "And if he did, then certain security measures are called for. Completely called for."

"I suppose so. But he didn't do it."

"We'll see."

Holman left my office, headed who knows where—maybe to smear more prints out at Anna Hocking's. And I waited, poring over what information the medical examiner had already sent to our office. It wasn't much. And now that the long night had worn the first flush of excitement from the chase, Martin Holman and I seemed to be the only ones still worried.

Deputies Paul Encinos and Tony Abeyta went back to the highway, looking for speeders—and no doubt flashing their spotlight into every damn field and yard, hoping for some more action.

Eddie Mitchell, an officer who was even less excitable than Bob Torrez, volunteered to sit out in Fuentes's driveway until we oldsters finally decided to do whatever it was that we were going to do.

I got the distinct impression that everyone in the department thought I was several cards short. Hell, I suppose the evidence agreed. We'd found a man blown to pieces in a field owned by a known crazy...and I was the one who was refusing to arrest our solitary suspect.

I saw Bob Torrez pass down the hallway and shouted at him.

"Estelle is on her way up, Roberto." I suppose I wanted at least one person on the staff to agree with me.

"I heard, sir."

The tall deputy stood in the doorway, a manila envelope under his arm.

"What are you working on?" I asked. I leaned back in the chair and hooked my hands behind my head. He lifted the envelope and gazed at it as if this were the first time he'd seen it.

"The arson investigator from Albuquerque sent back the second set of pictures I took of Sheriff Holman's house after the cleanup," he said. "I was going to go through them and see what he said."

I grimaced. The odds of us ever finding out who flipped the match were slim to none. I had given the case to Torrez because I knew he'd keep plugging. The case wouldn't end up at the back of a file drawer somewhere, covered with cobwebs.

"That and a million other things," I said. I took a deep breath and glanced out the doorway toward the dispatch room. "We may need your help this morning."

"Sure."

"Estelle and I will go out to talk with the old man. I don't want a damn contingent following us out there."

Torrez nodded and I added, "Maybe you can think of something to keep Holman busy if he shows up here in the office again. I really don't want him out there. Or the press either, for that matter. You may want to run out to the Hocking place again with him...it wouldn't hurt to look around again. See if we missed anything."

"He may want to see these photos," Torrez said, clearly thinking that the Hocking case was closed tight. I could imagine him methodically explaining each photograph to Martin Holman. The sheriff would love it, even if the photos showed next to nothing.

"That'll be fine. And by the way, I talked with Mrs. Sloan yesterday afternoon. I forgot to tell you."

Torrez looked uncomfortable. "I had some things I was going to do on that case today, but we sort of got...ah, busy."

"Well, I can save you some legwork, then. She said the main man went to live with his father in Florida."

"Todd Sloan? He went to Florida?"

"That's what she said."

Torrez frowned.

"What's the matter? As the old joke goes, his leaving raises the average IQ of both places."

Torrez almost grinned. "That means she and Kenny Trujillo are the only ones living in that trailer, then."

"I suppose so. Kenny was still at work when I talked with Miriam. She'd just come back from a trip to Albuquerque."

"Huh," Torrez said, still frowning. "Well, maybe."

"Well maybe what?"

"Well, I stopped by the discount store and talked with a couple people. One of the salesladies remembers Todd and three of his friends in the store during the earlier part of the week. She thought one of them was shoplifting, but she didn't say anything because she wasn't sure. Anyway, she says Todd Sloan bought a pair of tennis shoes."

"The same kind as in your photograph?"

"The same kind. Same size. Same everything. And the lack of wear on the ones in the photo would compare with some only a week old."

"Thin, Robert. Thin."

Torrez smiled. "But maybe enough to get him to talk."

"Except he's in Florida now. And I don't think you're going to win an extradition for tennis shoes."

Torrez took a step nearer the desk. "But I think she's lying for him again," he said. "You said that she claims he moved a couple weeks ago? This was Monday, when he was in the store. So he didn't move...at least not until just a few days ago."

"Mothers of teenagers are easily confused," I said. "But it would be convenient to move right after the burglary."

"That's what I was thinking."

"Well, keep thinking. Go out to the junkyard and talk with Kenny Trujillo. Maybe he needed a new engine hoist, so Todd obliged. You might ask Kenny when Todd moved to Florida. It might be interesting to compare his date with Miriam's. You'll get your chance to nail the little bastard. I'm sure that after a week or so, the juvenile authorities in Florida will be more than glad to send him back." Torrez almost grinned.

Unlike Bob, I didn't have a myriad of little details from other cases to look after—or at least none that I cared to bother with at the moment. By the time fifteen more minutes had passed, I had reached the limit of my patience. My hand kept straying to my shirt pocket, hoping to find an orphaned cigarette.

Finally I gave up. I walked out to the dispatcher's room and Randy Ames, one of our part-timers, swiveled his chair around at my approach.

"Morning, sir."

"I suppose. You got a cigarette?"

"No, sir. I sure don't. I don't smoke."

"Good. Don't start." A convenience store was kitty-corner from the department parking lot, across the street. I headed for that, and almost made it. Just as I was about to step off the curb, the only vehicle on Bustos Avenue turned from the eastbound lane and pointed its flat nose at me.

I recognized the blue Isuzu Trooper. I grinned widely when I saw that Estelle Reyes-Guzman had brought her entire family with her. Dr. Francis Guzman swung into the parking lot with the easy familiarity of an old-time employee. He pulled into a space marked Reserved for Sheriff.

On those rare occasions of a Gastner family reunion, my eldest daughter Camille was expert at those all-encompassing bear hugs that squeezed out what little breath I had. Camille was twice this slip of a girl's weight, but Estelle always managed to surprise me. She hugged me so hard one of the ballpoint pens in my shirt pocket cracked. And she did it while holding my godson in one arm.

"I was just headed over to the store," I said.

She pushed away and looked me up and down. "We'll walk over with you."

"That's okay. It wasn't important. God, it's good to see you."
Francis ambled around the front of the Trooper, a wide grin on
his handsome, swarthy face.

"Hey, *Padrino*," he said, and we shook hands. "You're lookin'
good."

Estelle grinned and wrinkled her nose. "You're still not
smoking." She saw the expression on my face and added, "But if
we'd had been ten minutes later, you would have started again,
right?"

"Five," I said. "It's been one of those days." I reached out and
moved the blue knitted shawl away from the baby's head. He was
sound asleep. "You know this is the first time this kid and I have
met?"

"And at work, too," Francis said with a laugh. "What a start."

"He's a good-looking boy." I frowned. "Were you planning
to—" I waved a hand. "I mean, do you want to take him over to
my house now, or what?"

"He's fine. Really. He'll be just fine. We really do need to talk, sir."

"Then let's head out to Reuben's. I'll fill you in on the way." I
immediately felt like a louse. I hadn't seen Estelle since the previous
August. And now, she'd been out of her truck for two minutes
and I had her working for Posadas County again.

"And let's take your truck," I said, starting toward her Isuzu.

"I don't have this county frequency on my radio," Estelle said,
but I didn't need reminding.

"I've got the handheld," I said, knowing damn well that it
wouldn't receive out in the rumpled country west of town. That
was all right. There were only three people in the world I wanted
to talk with just then—and two of them were the parents of my
godson. I had been surprised, at first, to see Francis. I guess I had
been expecting Estelle to arrive alone.

That was foolish. Estelle wasn't about to leave her infant son
in Mexico in someone else's care. And circumstances being what
they were, Dr. Francis Guzman's presence might prove useful, since
the third person I wanted to talk with was a cranky ninety-year-
old Mexican who didn't know his world was about to shatter into
a million pieces.

I had absolute faith that Reuben Fuentes would not be able to
hide anything from his grandniece. She would coax the story out

of him, one version or another. And if he was guilty, she'd tell me that, too. It was one of those times when I found myself wishing that Estelle Reyes-Guzman wasn't so damn unflinchingly honest.

17

I had to admit to a little impatience. When two cops get together, it's easy for them to jump in a patrol car and blast off in a cloud of exhaust and tire smoke. But not so when the entire family is involved.

Estelle took her time making sure the tiny, slumbering Francis Carlos Guzman was securely belted into his form-fitting, high-tech, plastic/Velcro/fiberglass infant car seat. The kid sure didn't care. He'd obviously inherited his father's easygoing pace.

Dr. Guzman took the wheel with me riding shotgun and Estelle in back with the baby. I twisted around in my seat and grinned at my sleeping godson. He had a round, fat face framed with fine, black hair. "A good-lookin' kid," I said again. Estelle smiled her inscrutable smile and let the sleeping child grip her little finger in his miniature fist.

Outside, the day was glowering, the sky still leaden and the wind raw and piercing. Snow in southwestern New Mexico was a rarity. When it came, it seldom lasted more than a few hours. But when I looked out of the Trooper, Minnesota would have been a good guess...or even Cleveland, where my youngest daughter lived.

New Mexico was supposed to be blank blue skies, so achingly clear that five minutes outside would start the skin cancer blooms for sure. The sun on a December high noon should be frying the retinas. But no. It was bleak and gray. The front was settling in with no significant weather predicted. Just mush. Depressing, gray mush.

"Have you talked with Reuben since they found the body?" Francis asked.

"Yes," I said. "As I told Estelle, the old man says he heard a couple of shots, but didn't go investigate."

"Then he's sure not feeling up to snuff," the physician said. He glanced at Estelle in the rearview mirror. "Ten years ago, he would have been out the door, shooting."

"He's not that bad," Estelle said.

"And no ideas who might have done it?"

I shook my head and Francis sighed. "This is going to be hard on him."

We rode in silence the rest of the way. During the jouncing ride up Reuben's two-track, the baby released his grip on Estelle's finger, turned his head toward the window, sighed deeply, and continued blowing Z's. He was as calm as they come. Hell, if all babies could be like that, I might not have settled for just four.

Francis parked the Isuzu within a dozen feet of the cabin. "Why don't I stay out here with the baby. Holler if you need me," he said. Estelle hesitated, then nodded.

I followed her toward the front door of Reuben Fuentes's dismal shack, one shoulder hunched against the wind.

The old man didn't answer the first knock, or the second.

"Is it locked?" I asked, and Estelle tried the latch. The door swung in with a protest.

"Reuben?" Estelle called. Her voice was musical, a wonderful contralto that could charm even old men who didn't care any more.

A small voice responded from somewhere inside. Estelle pushed the door fully open and I followed her in. Reuben Fuentes was sitting in his rocking chair in the corner, the same tiny bulb in the table lamp trying its best. He didn't rise.

Estelle crossed through the hodgepodge of litter in a couple of long-legged steps and knelt beside her granduncle. I closed the door against the wind and waited. I understood basic Mexican, words like *sí* and *gracias* and *de nada*, when they were spoken slowly and clearly by gringos. What passed between Estelle and her uncle, most of it spoken in low, urgent tones, reminded me of what butterfly wing beats might sound like if our ears were sharp enough to hear.

My eyes adjusted to the light and I saw that Estelle was holding the old man's hands in hers, but that the index and middle fingers of her right hand were touching the inside of his wrist.

She asked him a brief question with the word *médico* buried in it, and he shook his head wearily. That prompted her to lift a hand and run her fingers lightly down his wrinkled, leathery cheek. I heard the name *Francisco*, but that brought no response. I doubted if the old man knew who her husband was—maybe he didn't even remember that she was married.

She tried every argument there was, but the old man was adamant. Whatever was bothering him, he wanted no part of *médico*, *Posadas*, or *enfermedad* anywhere but in his own diggings.

Eventually they reached a quiet impasse. Reuben Fuentes sat hunched like a small, withered gnome, his head turned slightly away and his face in the shadows. Estelle sat on the floor at his feet, her hands and his in Reuben's lap.

I had no hint of how long this silent dialogue might continue but I had no intention of interrupting. My knees were beginning to protest standing so long. I pushed the old cat off one of the straight chairs and sat down. I could wait. I tried to survey the contents of the room, but the light was too dim.

The heat was almost oppressive as a great, gnarled piece of piñon smoldered in the fireplace. I unbuttoned my jacket, thinking that a blast of cold air through the door might feel good. After a few minutes of the warm silence, my eyes began to grow heavy-lidded, and I found myself wishing that Estelle would make up the old man's mind just a tad faster.

As if he'd heard my thoughts, Reuben Fuentes straightened a little, sighed, and patted the back of Estelle's hand. He said distinctly, "*Lo que paso, paso, Estelita.*"

"*No es necesario tío de mi abuela. Estoy aquí ahora.*" Her tone was tinged with impatience.

"*Está mejor...dejarme en paz, nina.*"

She placed a hand on his knee and used him as leverage to push herself to her feet. I thought I heard a joint crack and couldn't imagine this girl old enough for such things. Maybe she'd pushed too hard on Reuben's frail, razor-thin knee.

"*Bobo, bobo,*" she said softly, and she again took his hands in hers. I could see she was pulling him out of the chair, much the way a child, eager for play time, would tug at a recalcitrant adult. He gave in finally and pushed himself out of the chair.

It was as if ten years had passed since my last visit. The old man who hours before had been almost steady if not spry on his feet now stood wavering before his next step.

I got up, unsure of what either Estelle or Reuben intended.

"He'll go into town to see a doctor if we'll take him to the field first," Estelle said.

"You're ill, Reuben?" I asked. The answer was obvious, but I wanted the old man to talk to me, to recognize my presence.

"No, not so much," the old man replied. His voice was husky and forced. "But my niece, here—" He shook his head. "Can't leave an old man in peace."

"Yes, he is ill, sir." She tapped the center of her own chest with an index finger and shook her head.

"You want an ambulance to meet us at the county road?"

"No. He won't do that. I think he'll be all right if we just take it real slow. Francis has his medical bag in the car if we need it."

She ushered Reuben toward the door, stopping for a moment to wrap his sheepskin coat tightly around him. He looked at me, the ghost of a smile wrinkling the corners of his eyes.

"Are you finished with my field?"

"I think so, yes."

"Good. You know—" he drifted off for a second, then said, "my wife is buried down there, you know."

"I didn't know that." In fact I did know that his wife had been laid to rest in All Saints' Cemetery in Posadas a decade before, but who knew what ghosts had played in the old man's mind since then.

"She is. She told me not to go down there. That's why I didn't come to answer your questions."

"My questions?"

He lifted his bony shoulders in that slight, characteristic Mexican shrug of dismissal. "You and the others—"

"We need to get him out to the car," Estelle said, and the two of us all but carried the fragile old man to the Isuzu.

"I'll get in first, sir," Estelle said, and climbed in so she was sitting between the sleeping baby and Reuben. Francis reached back and touched Reuben's hand as the old man settled into the seat and I closed the door.

"*Don Reuben*," he said. Reuben Fuentes looked at him as he might a friendly stranger and said nothing.

"He wants to see the field first," I said. "There's a turnoff just down the path a bit. It takes us right out to the pasture without having to walk in from the road."

Francis didn't argue or press the moment with Reuben. He turned around with a quick glance at me and a raised eyebrow, then started the truck. In a moment we were jouncing back out the two-track.

Just beyond the first wash a faint path bore off to the left. Following Reuben's whispered directions, we turned off the worn path and nosed through brush and scrub.

Occasionally an oak twig would etch its way along the truck's paint, and I glanced back at Estelle.

She and the old man were deep in another of their private, silent conversations.

In less than fifty yards the brush fell away and we entered the northeast corner of the big pasture, a field that sloped down to the county road almost a quarter of a mile distant.

I pointed toward the west. "We want to head right for that outcropping down there, Francis. Right where the grove of oaks is the thickest." He threaded the truck between rocks and cactus, making way toward the west side of the pasture where the oak grove formed a necklace around the bottom of the limestone outcropping.

The jouncing finally awakened young Francis Carlos. He blinked awake, yawned mightily, said, "Ummmm," and settled in again.

"This is the spot," I said and Francis pulled to a stop a dozen paces from the gravesite. I glanced down toward the county road and saw that Eddie Mitchell's county car was still parked in Reuben's two-track. Since we had approached from the rear, the deputy obviously hadn't seen us...he wouldn't have recognized the Guzmans' truck, and would certainly have been prompted to action by the sight of someone driving through the field of evidence.

"Yes," Reuben said behind me. "I remember this spot." As well he should, I thought, since he had buried his three dogs in this hole not a week before. "I want to get out."

"You shouldn't, Tio. Just tell us about it."

"This is where I buried my dogs," he said.

"I know, Tio."

"They were poisoned."

"Yes."

"The man who did that...he was...*cobarde*. The dogs never hurt anybody."

He leaned forward and I saw that he was looking through the windshield at the disturbed earth. The grave was still open, the mound of dirt just visible.

"We took the bodies for tests, Reuben," I said. "We wanted to know what kind of poison killed the dogs. Maybe that way we can find who did it."

"*Cobarde*," he repeated.

I turned to Estelle. "Does he know who did it? Did he say?"

"I don't think so."

"Why don't you talk to me," Reuben said. His voice was stronger, fueled with indignation that I considered him so infirm that I would speak as if he weren't present.

"All right," I said. "Who killed your dogs, Reuben?"

He mumbled something and looked off toward the east. I watched him, finding it difficult to believe that a week ago this frail old man had dug a hole nearly eighteen inches deep and a yard square.

"I buried them myself," he said and I knew then that that would be the extent of his story. "I want to get out of the car."

This time, Estelle didn't protest, and Reuben moved as if he were tapping some last reserve of energy. He walked around the open door, putting a hand on the truck's fender for support with Estelle at his other elbow. I knew we were humoring him, probably pointlessly so. But in his mental wanderings, some small kernel of information might surface, might be of use.

He stood in the wind and the cold at the edge of that sorry hole in the ground and looked down at the fresh earth.

"This is it," he said.

"I don't want you catching cold, Tio." Estelle reached over and pulled his collar up higher.

"This is where I buried my dogs," he repeated. "Right here." He turned to look at me. "You could have just asked me."

"I did ask, Reuben," I said gently.

"If you had asked me, I would have told you the dogs were here." I let that pass without comment. I trusted Estelle's instinct about how much to push the old man's memory.

"Why did you dig so deep?" he asked.

"What do you mean?"

He gestured with considerable irritation. "So deep. *Por Dios.* It took me two hours to scratch the earth, and *mira.* You dig this *caverna.* What did you think you would find?"

I shrugged. "We removed the animals, that's all. When the lab is finished, we'll...we'll put them back. We'll rebury them."

"Good." His single word came out flat and final. He turned toward the truck. "*Tómame a casa, Estelita. Me canso del viento.*"

We did leave then, but it wasn't to take Reuben home. Instead, we drove him to Posadas General Hospital. He spent the rest of the day with an oxygen tube in his nose and strange chemicals dripping into the blue vein of his left arm. Francis slipped into his world of medicine as effortlessly as if he were a resident.

We hadn't been at the hospital for more than twenty minutes before Sheriff Martin Holman tracked us down and had me paged to the telephone. He kept his ranting to a minimum. It took me only five minutes to convince him that the drip tubes stuck in Reuben's arm weren't long enough to allow the old man to reach Mexico.

18

There was nothing Estelle or I could do for Reuben Fuentes at Posadas General Hospital. Dr. Francis Guzman settled into an endless round of conferences with the medical staff. What there was to talk about, I didn't know. Reuben's condition seemed simple enough to me.

The old man was comatose, drifting up to consciousness only fleetingly and never lucid. I was no medical expert, but I could see that he was simply worn out.

We had been at the hospital for an hour when Francis walked back into Reuben's room. He touched Estelle on the elbow and she stepped away from the bed. I was sitting in one of those extraordinarily uncomfortable vinyl lounge chairs in the corner, reading the "Humor in Uniform" section from a three month old *Reader's Digest*. I held the magazine in my right hand while cradling the little bundle that was a snoozing Francis Carlos with my left. I didn't get up.

"Why don't you two go get some dinner," he said.

"Us three, you mean," I said and laid the magazine down. The infant stirred, yawned, and wrinkled his nose and eyebrows...an expression I'd seen a hundred times on his mother's face. He fixed huge, luminous brown eyes on my old, wrinkled mug.

Francis thrust his hands in his trouser pockets in that characteristic gesture he used when he knew he had to be patient with other people perhaps not as efficient as himself.

Estelle raised an eyebrow and Francis continued, "I've arranged a meeting with Dr. Perrone and Fred Tierney for about five-thirty...it's the only time I could get the two of them together. I'll join you as soon as I can." Fred Tierney was the hospital administrator. It was easy to imagine that he was a little nervous about having the law hanging out in his facility.

"Is there anything we can do?" Estelle asked.

Francis shook his head. "Go eat." Estelle smiled at her husband and kissed him lightly on the cheek as she stepped past him.

"I thought maybe they'd make you wait," she said. He shrugged and shook his head. I didn't know what she was talking about and didn't pry. Estelle reached for her son and I gave him up so I could struggle out of the low chair. We left the hospital, planning to return after dinner.

We ate at the Juan de Oñate Cantina on 12th Street, one of Estelle's favorite haunts in Posadas. The place was dark and ornate, a miniature version of what someone thought a palace in Mexico City might have looked like in 1600. Little Francis Carlos fussed a bit at the darkness and strange smells until his mother let him put a stranglehold on a bottle.

We could have eaten the dinner, generous though it was, in fifteen minutes. But we first waited for Francis and then after he arrived, shortly after six, the three of us spent more than two hours dawdling over the food and catching up on gossip.

Finally, I pushed away the half-full basket of *sopaipillas* and my empty coffee cup. If I had eaten any more, I'd have been comatose and under the good doctor's care myself.

"You want to go out to the field tomorrow?"

Estelle frowned. It was the first time in more than an hour that I'd brought up the incident that had summoned her to Posadas. "Yes, sir."

"Pretty bleak place," Francis said. He reached across and pulled the *sopaipillas* within reach. He'd eaten more than I had, which was an accomplishment...especially since he didn't have the stretched belly capacity.

"You saw most of what there was to see this afternoon, when we took Reuben there," I said. "A hole in the ground, a few bloodstains." I held up my hands. "No nifty tire tracks pressed into the ground, no cartridge casings, no nothing."

"None of it makes sense," Estelle said.

"No. But there's a lot of that going around here lately." She didn't ask me what I meant by that and I didn't elaborate.

We left the restaurant and swung by the hospital for a few minutes. Reuben was sleeping quietly, looking tiny and defenseless under the white sheets. They'd given him a bath, probably more out of self-defense than anything else. The monitor over his bed ticked its record of his diminishing vital signs.

After a few minutes we headed for my adobe house on Guadalupe Terrace, deep in the old section of Posadas south of the interstate. The place was huge, sprawling, dark, and comfortable. And it was private, nestled almost in the geographic center of five acres.

Estelle paused a minute with her hand caressing the carved oak of the front door. Francis stood behind her, his son nestled in the crook of his arm.

"What are you thinking?" I asked.

"I'm thinking…I'm thinking that this feels like coming home."

I nudged the door open. "Someday you'll be able to talk some sense into your husband's thick skull. You and Francis need to get out of those gloomy mountains and come back south, where you belong."

Estelle laughed and shot an amused look at the young physician. They followed me inside. The old hacienda sprawled all over the lot with a myriad alcoves, nooks, and patios. Every member of a big family would have been able to find a quiet, private corner.

It was all of those rooms that prompted my two sons and two daughters to harass me about being lonely and "rattling around in that old barn," as my eldest daughter Camille was fond of saying.

I gave Estelle and Francis their choice of five bedrooms. She chose the one in the west wing, the bedroom with the dark, looming, mahogany *armario*. Camille had fallen in love with that old free-standing Mexican clothes closet when she was only thirteen. Two other deputies and I had nearly busted guts moving it in. It was never going to be moved again—not in my lifetime, anyway.

Estelle tossed her small overnight bag on Camille's bed. "You want the shutter open?" I asked.

"No. Leave it closed," she said. "I like the fortress effect." She smiled a little ruefully and slipped an arm around Francis. "I'm feeling small right now, sir. It's one of those times when a warm burrow is tempting."

"That's why I like this place. The rest of the world doesn't exist when you close the doors and windows." I started to swing the bedroom door closed behind me. "I'll fix us a brandy when you're ready."

They settled the kid and then found me out in the kitchen. Estelle stepped down onto the brick floor of the living room and wandered around the room like a little kid, poking into this and that. She stopped at the VCR and examined the single tape, the crow's feet at the corners of her eyes deepening. She knew me pretty well.

I handed Francis a brandy and he flopped down in one of the leather chairs, one leg thrown across the arm. Estelle sat down on the other arm of the same chair, hands folded primly on her knees. "Francis and I would like a place like this someday," she said.

"You won't find them up north," I chided her, and she grinned again. Anyone but Estelle would have told me to shut up and mind my own business.

We talked until nearly midnight, and after a while it seemed to me that she had never been gone.

※ ※ ※

The next morning, we drove to the hospital and found no change in Reuben's condition. He was still unconscious and it seemed to me, looking at the composed, peaceful expression on his pale face, that he had already made up his mind and was simply waiting for his body to follow suit.

Doctor Allen Perrone stuck his head in, beckoned to Francis, and nodded curtly at me. I wasn't going to let him get away with that. "So what do you think?" I asked, keeping my voice in a hoarse whisper. He glanced at Francis, shrugged, and summed up his medical prognostication in two vague, unhelpful words: "No telling."

He took Francis by the elbow and said to Estelle, "I need to borrow him for a bit."

"We were going to go out to Reuben's place for a little while," she said. "We should be back in a couple of hours."

We drove out to the field in my Blazer. Francis Carlos was blabby all the way, gurgling and cooing and twisting his rubbery little face into a wide range of expressions, each one sillier than the last.

Deputy Tom Mears, a part-time officer we had hired away from Bernalillo County after he'd stopped a 9 mm slug in the gut, was parked in Reuben's driveway. He lifted a finger in salute as we pulled beyond the driveway and parked along the road.

In daylight, the field looked considerably smaller than it had during the raw, unsettled night.

"You don't want to leave him in the truck?" I asked, as Estelle bundled the infant into a convenient package.

"No."

"You want me to carry him?"

"He's fine," she said. And he was. Once fitted into a gadget that looked like a high-tech cross between a hiker's backpack and a backboard for a papoose, the kid rode along in style. Estelle Reyes-Guzman shoved her hands in her pockets and followed me across the rough ground.

We stopped at the spot where Stuart Torkelson had fallen for the last time, and from there I pointed out where the small marker flags had been set by each site of evidence.

"Would you characterize the argument between my great-uncle and Stuart Torkelson as violent, sir?"

"When they met that first time? No. The way Torkelson told it, Reuben waited for him to walk to the fence. They exchanged a few words, and Torkelson backed off."

"And he admitted to you that he'd been in the wrong?"

"Absolutely. He was apologetic." I pulled my coat a little tighter. The wind hadn't given up. Another day of overcast would bring the total to three in a row...about all I could stand.

"It's hard to believe he would poison Reuben's dogs."

"Impossible for me to believe it," I said.

Estelle walked to the edge of the shallow pit and knelt down. I did the same, at considerable expense.

She looked up at the trees that surrounded us on three sides. "A pretty spot."

"Yes."

She reached down and picked up a handful of loose dirt from the edge of the hole, rolling it between her fingers. "How much deeper down did you dig...I mean after you reached the bodies?"

"Bob Torrez did most of the digging. He stopped when all three dogs were exhumed and when he was sure that that's all there was in the pit."

For a long minute she didn't respond, then she nodded once, as if what I had said was somehow suspect. "It's interesting, isn't it, sir." She pointed by moving just her index finger while the other fingers held onto the ball of soil.

"What is?"

"The way soil makes layers as it's formed."

Goddamned fascinating, I almost said, but a loud bark of radio squelch interrupted me. I grunted upright and turned around in time to see another county car pull to a halt behind my Blazer. I reached around and pressed the mike button on my handheld to let Torrez know we'd seen him.

"Can you come to the car a minute, sir?" Torrez's voice was restrained. I clicked the handheld again as acknowledgment. Scanner nuts around the county would wonder what the hell kind of conversation we were having.

"Let's go see what he wants," I said. As we walked back toward the road, Tom Mears got out of his unit to join us.

Deputy Torrez opened his briefcase on the hood of the car and had a handful of show-and-tell by the time Estelle and I negotiated the fence.

"What's up, Robert?"

"Some interesting findings came in from preliminary tests, sir." He handed me a single piece of paper with the letterhead of the office of the medical examiner.

"Huh," I said after reading the first paragraph. "Huh." I handed the paper to Estelle.

"Human blood was found on the fur of one of the dogs," Torrez said.

"So I read." I waited until Estelle had finished.

"And it's type B positive."

"The same as Stuart Torkelson's," Estelle added.

"Shit," I said and turned to lean against the fender of the county car. "They got that information back to us in record time, I'll say that. We might wait a month for the rest."

"There wasn't very much blood found," Estelle said. She reread the brief report for the fifth time. I didn't need to see it again.

"One molecule is all it takes," I said. I looked at Estelle as she handed the paper back to Torrez. "So tell me," I said.

"If the lab report is correct," Estelle said slowly, "and if the final analysis—the DNA fingerprint and all—agrees, then it places Torkelson with the dogs."

"Uh-huh." I reached over and took the report. "And you read the rest?"

"Yes, sir."

I held the paper at arm's length, not bothering to take the time to fish my glasses out of my pocket. "Item 93-1216PC10...blood sample recovered from collar fur of deceased black and tan female collie-cross canine." I glanced up. "That's a bit redundant, isn't it?"

Estelle raised an eyebrow.

I continued reading. "Blood sample typed as B Rhesus positive, preliminary match with Item 93-1216PC06, sample taken from victim identified as Stuart Torkelson."

"Yes, sir."

"And," I said, holding the paper another inch farther away, "blood sample obtained from splash pattern measuring approximately two point seven centimeters by eight point eight centimeters on left rib cage of canine. Blood sample contaminated by soil and soil debris located between sample and animal fur."

Estelle thrust her hands back in her pockets.

"What's that tell us?" I prompted when I saw the line of her jaw set.

"It's hard to tell, sir."

"No, it isn't, Estelle."

"Somehow Torkelson's blood got sprayed on the dog when its fur was already covered with dirt," Bob Torrez offered.

"Somehow," I said and handed him the paper. "Estelle, your great-uncle loved his dogs. He buried them here, and the effort will probably end up killing him. The dogs were already covered with dirt when Torkelson was shot. That doesn't leave many choices."

"Like they were just in the process of being buried," Bob Torrez offered.

"Or being exhumed. That's the opposite possibility."

"Maybe, sir," Estelle said.

"Then you tell me."

"I can't, sir."

"There's one thing that can't be changed. Torkelson's blood type is on one of the dogs. That's a link we didn't have before."

"A link?"

"Yes. Until now, it was just supposition that tied Torkelson's death to your uncle. This makes the connection more tangible."

"Even if we don't know how to read the evidence," Estelle said with considerable acid in her voice.

"Even if." I turned to Torrez. "Did Holman see this?"

"Yes, sir."

"*Va a arruinar esta investigación*," Estelle muttered and I held up a hand.

"Stop that."

"I said he's going to make a mess out of this case, sir. He's so damn eager to pin this murder on an old man."

"I don't think that's it. But he wants something. He's got a lot of people breathing down his neck on this one. Torkelson was as close to being a town father as anyone can get. We can't afford to sit around, waiting for something to break."

"We're not going to do that, sir," Estelle said with a finality that I had long ago learned to accept as damn close to marching orders.

"What do you suggest?"

"We're going to talk with my great-uncle."

"That may not be possible."

"It's going to have to be, sir."

19

Reuben Fuentes was waiting for his grandniece. That's the only way I could describe it. We reached the hospital and entered through a side service door. We had to pass the main nurses' station to reach the old man's room, and Evelyn Bistoff cast a glance our way, nodded brightly at me, and then ignored us.

The door of Room 118 was ajar. I could see Reuben from the hallway. His usually tousled, snow-white hair was neatly combed, almost a halo, and his head was turned so he could see out into the hall.

The expression on his face said that he'd been expecting us. I had expected to see Francis Guzman in attendance, but the young physician wasn't there.

Over the years, both Estelle Reyes-Guzman and I had endured our share of death-bed scenes where the victim gave a final statement of affairs as his fading brain understood them. The statements usually weren't allowed in court, but that didn't stop the process. Sometimes valuable information was uncovered, sometimes not. Most often, it was just an experience that left everyone with a little more of an ache, feeling a little more mortal, than before.

I had considered suggesting that Deputy Torrez accompany us. We could rely on him as a neutral third party. He could run the tape recorder and even ask the tough questions that make us all flinch.

But I didn't do that. I decided this time to follow the lead of Estelle's intuitions.

She walked to the side of the bed and took one of Reuben's skeletal hands in hers.

"¿*Como estás ahora, mi tío?*"

Reuben didn't let Estelle's hand go, but he waved the other hand in my direction. His eyes were bright and amused.

"That old gringo there doesn't speak Mexican, Estelita," he said. His voice was husky and soft, but he spoke with a clarity that startled me.

"*Que lástima,*" Estelle said, and we both laughed. Reuben even managed a weak smile, showing the brown tips of his three remaining teeth.

"Your husband was just here," he said. "He said to tell you that he would be right back."

"That's fine, tío. You're feeling better?"

The old man shrugged by just moving his eyebrows. He didn't release her hand. "They will blame me, is that it?" Reuben said without preamble. I stepped closer to the bed. I had no idea how long his lucidity would last and wanted to make the most of it.

"We don't have anything to go on, Reuben," I said. "Nothing. We need information."

"Yes."

Estelle sat on the edge of the bed. "Tío, when the dogs were poisoned...did you see or hear anything?"

Reuben shook his head. "The one dog, Lucy. She came back to the house, Estelita. I heard her. I went to look and found her under the truck."

"And that's all?"

"Yes."

"And the night of the shooting? You didn't go down to the field?"

"No."

"Why not?"

"I didn't feel so good, Estelita. I thought about it. And then I decided...well," and he picked at the hem of the sheet with his free hand. "I have no cattle any more, so if it was hunters after the deer—" he shrugged again. "What could I do?"

"So the first you knew of the shooting was when I came to visit after the body was found?" I asked.

"Yes." He smiled faintly. "And I wasn't feeling so good, señor sheriff. I wasn't feeling so good."

"Tío, yesterday when we went out to the field, you said something about the dogs' grave."

"I did?" Reuben looked puzzled, and he watched as Estelle dug into her black purse and retrieved a small brown notebook. It was one of those with graph paper pages and the word *Ideas* on the cover, favored by Forest Service types. She'd been in the mountains too long.

She flipped it open, searched briefly, and then read aloud, "You asked Señor Gastner, 'Why did you dig so deep?'"

Reuben's eyes shifted from the notebook to Estelle's face. "You write down what I say?"

"Sometimes, tío."

He digested that for a long minute, then asked, "Then what did I say?"

For a moment I thought he was joking, but the confusion in his eyes told me differently.

"You said that it took you two hours to scratch a hole for the dogs, and that we dug a cavern."

"I don't remember. But the soil was hard, no?" He looked at me. "Why did you take the dogs, señor?"

"To find out what killed them, Reuben."

"Somebody poisoned them. Did you know that?"

"Yes."

"Who was it, tío?"

"Who was it?"

"Yes. Who murdered your dogs?"

He frowned and patted the back of Estelle's hand. "It was a sad thing, you know." He smiled brightly and I could see the signals fading, the long moment of lucidity coming to a close. "How is the *niña*, Estelita?"

"Fine, tío. The *niño* is fine. It's a boy." The kid still rode in style, facing backward.

"That's good." He closed his eyes and Estelle and I watched silently as his body composed itself for another long session with limbo. Estelle finally put his hand down on the stark white sheet and moved away from the bed. She nodded toward the hall.

With the hospital room door closed behind her, she let out a long sigh. "I thought for a little while there that I was going to get my uncle back, sir."

I put an arm around her shoulders and gave both her and the papoose a squeeze. "I don't think it's in the cards," I said. "You want to stay here with him? So you're here when he wakes up again?"

She looked down at the floor. "I'm the only relative he has," she said. "He must feel terribly alone here."

"He's lived alone for years, Estelle."

"Out at the cabin. That's different. Not here." She looked up and down the sterile corridor. "I'm not even sure he knows where he is."

We heard footsteps on the polished tile and Sheriff Martin Holman turned the corner down by the nurse's station. He had Eddie Mitchell in tow, and the deputy looked embarrassed.

Holman was dressed in solid tan—the kind of cotton work pants and shirt the telephone company linemen like—with a denim jacket and a goddamned brown baseball cap with the Posadas County sheriff's department logo above the bill.

It was out of keeping with his usual neat business suit. Maybe he'd taken up coaching little league to improve his public image. A folded newspaper was tucked under one arm.

"Um," Estelle said, but kept it at that.

"Ms. Reyes-Guzman, good to see you again," Holman said. He smiled with some sincerity and extended a hand.

"Good to see you, sir."

"And is this the newest Guzman?" he said, stepping around so he could see Francis Carlos. The child had the good sense to be asleep again. "What a handsome child." Duty done, the sheriff turned to me. "So what's the deal?"

I held up a hand. "Reuben's in and out. We just talked with him for a few minutes. He doesn't know who poisoned his dogs, and he didn't do anything or see anyone when he heard the two shots. He wasn't feeling well."

"Ah," Holman said, nodding. I half expected him to pull a pen out of his pocket and begin sucking on it like Peter Sellers. "I thought it would be a good idea to have one of the deputies stay here."

"Oh? Why is that?"

"Well, security and all."

"Martin," I said, trying to keep my thinning patience intact, "Reuben Fuentes is not going anywhere. If he does regain consciousness again, he doesn't have the strength to turn over in bed, much less sprint for the door and grab a Greyhound for Juarez."

Holman smiled and winked at Estelle. "He's still as cranky as ever, isn't he? Bill, Mr. Fuentes heading for Mexico is not what worries me, Bill. The press is starting to flock."

I ignored his repetition of my name like an unctuous preacher. "What do you mean?"

"There's a newspaper reporter from Albuquerque and a television crew from Las Cruces down in the hospital waiting room right now. In addition to the locals. They'd be up here in a minute if we'd let them."

"We won't let them," I said flatly.

"Damn right," Holman agreed. "The old man's got little enough privacy as it is without the vultures at his doorstep." He pulled out the newspaper that he had had tucked under his arm and handed it to me. "Did you get a chance to see this yet?"

I unfolded the paper enough to see it was that day's edition of the *Posadas Register*. "What am I supposed to see?" The top stories were county legislature messes, sewer authority meetings, and a new roof for the middle school out at Crosby's Acres.

One more fold turned and there I was, fat belly, gray hair, and all. The picture had been taken at Anna Hocking's. The camera had caught me pointing with one hand while the other hand was on Deputy Tony Abeyta's shoulder. Were it not for the uniform and hardware, I would have looked like an aging football coach giving a pep talk to my star running back.

The headline, across all six columns, said, Serve and Protect More than Words.

"Read it. Take it with you and read it. Good stuff." Holman was grinning. "Makes you a hero, Bill. Won't hurt our budget one damn bit either." He turned to Mitchell. "You won't mind parking here for a little bit. Maybe just a couple hours? We'll have one of the part-timers relieve you as soon as we can."

"Yes, sir." The reply was crisp and professional, but I could see that Mitchell did mind.

"Bob Torrez was going to come, but he said he had a lead he needed to chase down. Sounds like he's going to nail the little bastard who burned down my house last summer."

It sounded to me like Torrez had been faster on the excuse draw than Mitchell. But whatever the motivation, the protection of old Reuben's privacy was a good move. I had to give Holman some credit.

"So what's next?" Holman said. He took me by the elbow and started escorting me down the damn hallway toward the nurses' station as if I were an aging, ambulatory patient heading for an enema session.

"We wait for the rest of the lab results to come back, I suppose," I said.

"That's it?" Holman had the grace to say it as a simple query, without any accusations.

"We're short on physical evidence, Marty. We're going to have to be very lucky. Whoever shot Stuart Torkelson didn't leave many tracks. No casings. No prints. No tire tracks...none that we can separate out, anyway. Clean job."

"What do we do, then...I mean, in a case like this?"

"We keep sifting. We hope something breaks."

Holman looked down at the polished tile floor for a minute and when he looked up, his mouth was pursed and his brow furrowed. He raised his right hand and slowly folded down his fingers until just the index was pointing heavenward. "Do we have a single, solitary bit of evidence that says the killer *wasn't* Reuben Fuentes?"

I wished that he hadn't asked me that. I took a long moment to frame my reply. "Just that common sense tells us Reuben isn't capable of that kind of violent, high-activity crime."

"I hope you're right," Holman said.

Estelle Reyes-Guzman touched my arm. "Sir, I'd like to visit with a couple people while I'm here. Maybe we could slip away now for a few minutes while Uncle Reuben's resting. If he needs anything, Francis is here. We could come back this afternoon."

I couldn't read in the dark depths of Estelle's eyes what she had in mind, but it wasn't visiting old friends. Holman let us escape any more questions from either him or the press, and when we were out in the parking lot, I grinned at Estelle.

"Visiting?" We climbed into my Blazer and I waited while she performed the ceremony of lashing in the papoose.

"Well, sort of," Estelle said. She glanced back toward the hospital. "I don't think we have a lot of time."

"No."

"Would you ask Bob Torrez to meet us back out at Uncle Reuben's?"

"Sure. What are you thinking?"

"Just something nagging." She turned around and looked in the back of the Blazer, then nodded.

"Estelle—"

"Sir?"

"You can talk to me. What's on your mind? What do you want to talk with Bob about?"

"I don't need to talk with him, sir. I need his expertise with a shovel."

20

Whatever it was that she was after, Estelle Reyes-Guzman didn't want to make it a production. She wanted just the three of us— four if I counted Francis Carlos. His forensic training was starting early, but he seemed plainly bored with the whole process.

She couldn't resist glancing at the newspaper article as we drove out to Reuben's. "Do you want to know what it says?" Estelle asked, and before I could answer she read the first paragraphs under Linda Rael's by-line.

> During the investigation into the death of an elderly Posadas County resident Friday night, Sheriff's Department personnel demonstrated that theirs is a job that goes far beyond the lifting of fingerprints, sifting of clues, or filing volumes of paperwork.
>
> "The victim has the right to privacy," says Undersheriff William G. Gastner. And his staff's protection of Mrs. Anna Hocking's property—and privacy—were evident that night.

Estelle looked over at me and grinned. "I thought your middle initial was K," she said.

"It is." She read the rest, the sort of thin stuff that small town papers like to print as their nod to public service. What it amounted to was a dozen column inches that explained why we hadn't allowed Miss Rael inside the Hocking house. No wonder Holman was pleased.

"You'll want to keep this for your scrapbook," she said when she finished.

"I don't have a scrapbook," I said. "And I can't wait for the second installment. I wonder how she's going to sanitize three dead dogs exhumed in the middle of the night after a prominent citizen and newspaper advertiser gets himself murdered. That ought to be a real challenge."

Deputy Robert Torrez was waiting for us when we reached Reuben's driveway. He took the shovel I handed him from the back of the Blazer.

"What are we looking for?" he asked. The shovel handle looked like a match stick in his big hands.

"I don't know," I said. We slipped through the fence. "What time did Holman call in Tom Mears?" The deputy's car was no longer parked in Reuben's lane.

"I heard him on the radio," Torrez said. "I think it was about two o'clock."

"The sheriff is confident," I said. We followed Estelle and Francis Carlos across the field.

"She takes him everywhere?" Torrez asked with the naive puzzlement of a true bachelor. Estelle pretended not to hear.

"Everywhere," I said.

The hole where the dogs had been buried was undisturbed. It was roughly three feet on a side, slightly rhomboid-shaped because of an outcropping of limestone that intruded a sharp corner into the grave.

"So, oh inscrutable one," I said, standing at the edge of the hole. "What are we looking for?"

Estelle got down on her knees and leaned as far down as she could without the papoose sliding over her head. She was looking closely at the dirt.

She pointed along the smooth vertical cut of one side. "I was looking at this earlier," she said. "You can see that the first six inches or so is really black on this side. Rich humus from recent accumulation of leaves. And then, as we go down," and she bent further and pointed, "the soil color changes considerably until by about fourteen inches down, it's much lighter brown...almost a dark golden color."

"Doesn't soil always do that?" I asked. "Get lighter and more leached out as you go down?"

"I would guess so. If we dug much deeper, we'd see other zones, maybe, and start getting into more rock. Maybe even pockets of sand."

"And so—"

"And so that's what I'd like to do." She knelt back on her haunches and brushed off her hands. She twisted, looking for something. She stretched to her right and grabbed a dead piece of juniper limb wood and used it like a chalkboard pointer.

"You see the dirt in the bottom of the grave, sir."

"Yes." I saw the dirt all right, but wasn't following her logic. "It's very dark…like surface soil."

I frowned and stared into the shallow pit. The soil on the bottom was indeed the same dark, rich humus as the first several inches.

"So maybe that was the first dirt thrown back in the hole after the dogs were buried," I said. Robert Torrez said nothing. He leaned on the shovel, one black boot on the tool's shoulder. Over the years, he'd heard Estelle and me supposing many times before. He was patient.

"No, for two reasons. First, if you dig a hole, the first dirt out is the last dirt back in, unless you make a conscious effort to line the dirt up so you can reach the—"

I interrupted her by holding up a hand. "All right. All right. I see that."

"And second, even if the person did that, the bodies of the dogs would separate the fill-in layer from the undisturbed soil underneath—the lighter colored soil."

"Estelle," I said. "Get a grip. When most people dig a hole, they toss dirt first one way and then another. One arm gets sore, they switch to the other. The dirt goes every which way, too."

"Exactly, sir."

"Are you following this, Robert?"

"No, sir."

"That's good. Otherwise I'd be worried."

"Sir, it's simple. When Uncle Reuben dug a hole for the dogs, he would stop when he thought the hole was deep enough. Right?"

"Yes. Or when he was exhausted."

"Of course. And when he stopped digging, what did he do?"

"He laid the dead dogs in the hole."

"Right. Regardless of how a person shovels dirt, or how his arms get tired, why would Uncle Reuben take the time to line the bottom of the hole with fresh topsoil?"

"He wouldn't." I looked into the hole again, uneasy. The bottom of the hole was certainly darker soil. It wouldn't take long to find out. "Robert, the shovel."

Torrez stepped into the hole gingerly, as if he were afraid that the floor was going to cave in. The first shovelful of dirt came out easily, but on the second probe, the clank of metal against rocks was loud.

The deputy grunted, dislodging several rocks. He worked for perhaps ten minutes, clearing out a corner so that he could stand away from a new area. He paused to take a breath and glanced at me.

Estelle stood on the opposite side of the hole from me, expressionless, arms across her chest. When Torrez paused, she said quietly, "See how those rocks aren't seated?"

"What do you mean?"

"If rocks have been in the ground for thousands—millions—of years, they take some persuasion to bust loose. And the dirt around them is compacted hard. Those rocks Bob just took out were part of the fill."

"Damn soil scientist now," I muttered, but I could see her logic was just common sense.

In another thirty minutes, Torrez had deepened the hole another foot and a half. And then his shovel hit serious rock. No matter where he drove the point, it met with the bright, sharp sound of Precambrian resistance.

"What do you think?" he said.

"Can you clean around one of the stones? One of the big ones?"

"They're all big," Torrez observed dryly. He choose a spot in the middle of the hole and cleaned the dirt away from a boulder that was nearly two feet long and a foot and a half wide. It was anyone's guess how thick the rock was.

"Are you sure about this?" I asked Estelle.

"I'm sure. Wait a minute." She turned and started across the field, then stopped. She looked at me, surprised. And then she grinned ruefully. "Sir, I was going to the car for my camera gear—"

卍 卍 卍

I laughed. "You forgot what county you're in, my dear. My camera bag is behind the passenger seat in the Blazer. I'll go get it. You're welcome to use it."

"I'll do it, sir." I tossed her the keys and she said to Torrez, "Don't go any deeper."

She set off toward the Blazer at a fast jog, the kid riding shotgun enjoying the hell out of police work. I think she'd forgotten Francis Carlos was there.

Torrez stepped up and out of the hole and once more leaned on the shovel. "She's betting that someone dug up the dogs, buried something underneath, and then reburied them," he said.

"Uh-huh," I said.

"The old man would never do a thing like that."

"No indeed."

"Do you think she's right?"

I shrugged. "We'll see."

Estelle returned with the camera bag and fished out my Pentax. She frowned at the numbers, turning the camera this way and that. I knew what she was looking for. I never remembered to put the end of the film box in the little bracket on the camera back.

"It's ASA four hundred," I said. Francis Carlos made a little whimpering sound and I added, "Let me hold Squirt."

"That would help," she said, and shrugged out of her backpack. I turned my back to the breeze, held the swaddled infant and made faces at him. His eyes got big, then narrowed, and finally he settled for a gurgle and a toothless smile.

Estelle adjusted the camera settings and shot half a dozen photographs of the grave from several angles. Then she said, "Bob, would you put the tip of the shovel right at the corner of that big rock. I need something for reference."

Torrez did so, posing the handsome shovel until Estelle was satisfied. "All right," she announced. "Go ahead and take out that stone."

"Says you," Torrez jibed. He was good-humored for someone that close to a shovel.

"No, it'll move easily," Estelle said. "Someone put those rocks in there. If they could move them and drop them in the hole, you can move them too. Probably easier."

Torrez took that as a compliment for his considerable strength. The tip of the shovel did indeed dislodge the rock. He pried one end up then kicked the shovel out of his way and bent down.

With a grunt he upended the stone.

"Oh, si," Estelle said.

As skeptical as I might have been, even I could see what excited her. The bottom of the rock—that portion that should have been in soil-packed darkness for eons—was covered with loose dirt, as one might expect. But clinging to the stone's surface was the multicolored lichen that dots most of New Mexico's exposed rock surfaces.

"Well, son of a bitch," I said and bent down. Francis Carlos let out a squeal and then a fretful monosyllable. I knew what that meant even before glancing down to see the puzzled look on his face.

"The lad committed an indiscretion," I said.

"He'll have to wait a minute," Estelle said. "I want pictures. Don't move it, Bob."

That left Deputy Torrez in an uncomfortable crouch, balancing the rock on its end. Estelle burned more film.

The lichen still displayed its potpourri of colors, from bright yellows to murky browns and russets. It hadn't been in the ground long.

"All right," Estelle said. She moved to one side as Torrez heaved the rock up and out of the hole. "Trade?" she said, holding out the camera. I gladly passed over the infant.

The capital murder investigation came to a fragrant halt as Estelle unswathed, cleaned, and changed the baby. It had been many years. I'd managed to forget that part.

Refreshed and heavy-lidded with accomplishment, Francis Carlos was once more deposited in my arms.

Estelle shot photos as Torrez worked, his pace stepped up by anticipation. He cleared an area nearly the width of the hole and another ten inches deep, a layer of jumbled rocks that evidently had been tossed into the grave after being gathered from the nearby flank of the mesa.

"We can search under the oaks over there and find the impressions where all these came from," Estelle said, but Torrez interrupted my reply.

"Something," he said. He dropped the shovel and crouched down, brushing with his bare hands. "It's plastic," he said. He pulled at a corner and we could see the black plastic, still glossy. Estelle took more pictures.

"What do you think, sir?" Estelle asked.

"I think this is a hell of a time to hesitate."

"Be careful, then," Estelle said, and Torrez nodded. He worked around the plastic, using hands and shovel with care. After a couple minutes he paused.

"This may be a corner," he said. "This is where part of the bag is tied off." He knelt down and worked on a knot. "It's more like a garden drop cloth," he added. "At first I thought it was a garbage bag, but the plastic's heavier."

"Here," I said, and extended my pocket knife toward him.

"No, I got it." He parted a corner of the plastic and recoiled. "Uh," he said with a grimace.

"Well, we know now someone didn't bury money or drugs out here," I said. Torrez was leaning away from the bag, holding the plastic at arm's length.

"Close it up until we finish uncovering the whole thing," I said. "Estelle, you want to go down to the car and call in? We'll want the coroner out here."

She looked at me quizzically and I realized I'd made the same natural mistake that she had.

"Forget it. I'll do it." I lateraled Francis Carlos over to his mother. By the time I returned, Bob had uncovered most of the bag. It appeared to be a piece of garden plastic about ten feet square. The plastic was tied around itself with no other ropes or twine visible. The body inside wasn't large.

"We don't want to move it yet," Estelle said. She reloaded the camera and took portraits of black plastic from every conceivable angle.

"After the coroner finishes, we'll lift it out," I said.

"We're covered. I've got plenty of shots."

Estelle's impatience was unusual, but I didn't argue. I couldn't recall a single case she had ever lost through faulty or incomplete evidence.

"All right. You ready, Roberto?"

"I guess."

We each took one end of the bundle and lifted it out of the hole, a grave now almost three and a half feet deep. The plastic-wrapped corpse landed with an unceremonious thud on the hard surface.

"So," I said. "Let's find out who we've got."

Robert Torrez drifted backward, away from the bundle. It was a moment when we could have used a stiff portion of New Mexico's wind. But the afternoon was dead calm.

21

Todd Sloan had run out of luck. He'd ended up stuffed in the ground under three dead hound dogs with nothing but a piece of garden plastic for a comforter.

With the plastic peeled back so that the pathetic, small corpse was completely exposed, Estelle Reyes-Guzman took photos and measurements. I stood back and wondered what to do next. Robert Torrez kept saying, "Huh," as if that one grunt summed it all up.

"His mother said he went to Florida to live with daddy," I said. "She said he went there a couple of weeks ago." Torrez nodded and offered his one syllable. "But you said he was at the shoe store earlier in the week, buying a pair of shoes that could tie him to the farm supply robbery."

"So either she was lying, or she really didn't know that he was still hanging out around town," Torrez said, finally slipping back into gear.

"She would know," Estelle said. She knelt down next to my briefcase and rewound an exhausted roll of film.

"Why is that?"

"She just would."

"A mother speaks," I said, and pulled a corner of the blanket away from Francis Carlos' face. He was sleeping through the best part.

"But it's true, sir," Estelle persisted. "If her son was in town, she'd know about it."

"Then there's only one alternative," I said.

"She was lying." I could see the artery in Deputy Torrez's neck pulse as his blood pressure escalated. He kept shifting position, trying to get away from the smell.

"Could be."

"There's a bigger question," Estelle said, standing up with a freshly loaded camera. She looked at me and raised one eyebrow.

"Does she know that her son is planted up here," I said.

"Right."

"Before all the fireworks start, we need to ask her. Robert, pick up Gayle Sedillos to act as a matron and go on out to the trailer park. Pick up Mrs. Sloan and bring her out here. She can identify the remains right here."

"Are you sure you want to do that, sir?" Estelle asked.

"Yes, I'm sure. If she doesn't know the boy's dead, we'll be able to tell." I looked at Torrez. "We'll meet you down at the road. Don't just lead her up here cold. I want a minute to talk with her first."

"Yes, sir."

"And Robert—"

"Sir?"

"I *do not* want the press up here. Not yet, anyway."

He nodded and trotted off toward his patrol car, glad for the fresh air.

"It would appear he was wounded twice, sir," Estelle said.

"Not heavy caliber, though?" I was thinking of Stuart Torkelson's run of bad luck.

"I would guess not. It looks like he was shot once here, behind the ear. It didn't rupture the vault of the skull, so we should be able to recover a slug. And it looks like he was wounded somehow in the stomach as well. There's a lot of blood there."

"The autopsy will tell us all we need to know." I took a deep breath and let it out slowly, wishing that I had a cigarette to clean up the fouled air. "You willing to make any guesses?"

"No, sir. I'm sure that Reuben had nothing to do with it. He couldn't have managed. And he wouldn't have bothered."

"Unless he had a partner," I said and watched the dark expression cloud Estelle's face.

"That's not a habit he would be apt to adopt this late in his life," she said, her tone clipped with annoyance. "He lived alone."

"Just mentioning all angles," I said. "That leaves two routes. Torkelson was into something that went sour. Something that involved the kid here. Or...Torkelson just happened to wander into the wrong place at the wrong time."

Estelle offered a slight smile. "I'm glad this isn't in my jurisdiction."

"You'd never guess it. And turnabout is only fair. I'll get you so wrapped up in this you'll never go home."

"You'd do that."

"Yes, I would." I looked down at Todd Sloan's sorry remains and was reaching down with my free hand to flip the plastic back over him when Estelle extended a hand to stop me.

"Wait a minute," she said. She knelt down, moving to keep her shadow out of the way. "I don't understand this. Look at his hair."

I did so and saw sandy blond hair caked with blood and dirt.

"And here," Estelle said, pointing at Todd Sloan's face around the eyes. "And here."

"And everywhere," I added. "He's covered with dirt."

Estelle nodded and rocked back on her haunches. "So tell me what I'm missing," she said.

"When a body is buried, it gets dirty," I said. "That might be one of the more predictable things in life."

Estelle shot me one of her rare withering looks. Behind us on the county road traffic was picking up. The ambulance arrived, with Dr. Emerson Clark's blue Buick not far behind. I knew the elderly physician would stay with his car until one of the officers arrived to escort him over the uneven ground...after they cut the barbed wire fence.

"Sir," Estelle said, ignoring the traffic. "Todd Sloan was wrapped in heavy plastic when he was buried here."

"I see that."

"It would protect the corpse from the dirt. Somewhat, at least."

I pushed the black plastic aside with the toe of my boot and looked at Todd Sloan again. "Well, son of a bitch," I said. And now that I looked, it was as obvious as daylight. The dirt—most of it pale dun yellow in color—was pressed into the clothes, the hair, even remnants of it here and there on Sloan's face. I bent over and looked closer. "I'll be damned."

"What do you think, sir?"

I looked up at Estelle. Her expression was worried. I couldn't fault her for that. I was worried too. Todd Sloan had been buried once without benefit of the plastic shroud. And then he'd been exhumed, stuffed in plastic, and reburied out here, on the edge of this desolate pasture. For the first time I realized how lucky old Reuben Fuentes had been. He hadn't heard anything. And he wouldn't have stood a ghost of a chance against the sort of person who'd killed Todd Sloan.

22

The efficiency of the Posadas community grapevine was astonishing. We were careful. Not once did I or one of my deputies slip and mention murder, corpse, burial, or Reuben Fuentes over the radio. Not once.

And yet, when Robert Torrez finally returned with Gayle Sedillos and Miriam Sloan in the back seat of his county car, he had difficulty finding a place to park. The narrow county road was a dusty bumper to bumper crowd scene.

And the press, damn its efficient hide, was there. Linda Rael had cornered Sheriff Holman, who didn't want to get anywhere near the burial site or the bagged corpse. He obviously wasn't giving Linda much satisfaction, because she kept looking our way—probably wondering who the stately Mexican woman in my company was. Or maybe she was wondering why the hell I was walking around holding a sleeping infant.

I handed Francis Carlos to his mother and headed for the roadway.

For his part, Holman kept looking up the road at a large white van with the Channel 3 logo on its side. He patted his hair for the tenth time, always ready should the unblinking eye turn his way. No one was going to cross the fence without my say-so. Tommy Mears had stretched a yellow crime scene ribbon along enough of the barbed wire that everyone got the point.

Torrez parked in the middle of the road and I reached the fence just as he opened the back door of the patrol car for Miriam Sloan and Gayle. Gayle, half Mrs. Sloan's age and as stylish as the other woman was frumpy, was dressed in civilian clothes. She expertly put herself between Mrs. Sloan and the burly youngster who balanced the large television camera on his shoulder.

Gayle and the deputy led Mrs. Sloan to the spot in the fence where we'd fashioned a narrow gate.

I met them there and reached out to take Mrs. Sloan by the elbow as she slipped past the loose wires.

"Sheriff," I said loudly enough for Martin Holman to hear. He'd been working his way toward us, trying to stay helpful to Linda and the dozen other curious onlookers at the same time. He excused himself, looking grateful.

Miriam Sloan was wearing a pale blue housedress and a worn cardigan sweater…no coat, typical of long-time New Mexicans who harbored that curious, innate belief that as long as the sun shone, it was shirt-sleeve time. Her shoes—more like slippers— were blue plastic and almost as inappropriate for the hike across the field as if she'd been barefoot.

She was breathing hard but otherwise her face was set in a stolid mask.

"We're sorry to have to bring you out here," I said, keeping my hold on her left elbow. Gayle flanked right, and to my surprise Miriam Sloan stepped right out, far more surefooted than I.

We said nothing as we crossed the field. A couple dozen feet from the grave site, I heard Martin Holman behind me say something like, "Hmmmmm," and I glanced over my shoulder. The sheriff was showing great interest in the limestone patch off to one side, where the first blood traces had been found. The smell had gotten to him.

Mrs. Sloan didn't hesitate. She stopped abruptly two paces from the grave, with the plastic-wrapped body within kicking distance.

Deputy Torrez had removed the small tape recorder from his shirt pocket. I noticed that Gayle's was clipped to her belt.

Torrez caught my glance and nodded that he was ready.

I said, "Mrs. Sloan, I know this is difficult for you." From the expression on her face I would have guessed that she'd find it more interesting to be home washing out empty mayonnaise jars. I stepped forward, bent down, and peeled back the corner of the plastic far enough that Todd Sloan's entire head and neck were visible.

"Mrs. Sloan, is this your son, Todd?"

I could have counted to five in the heavy silence that hung around us. Then she said, "Yes."

I snapped the plastic back in place and stood up. "We appreciate you coming out. I'm sorry." There wasn't much else to say to her, at least nothing that would make her feel any better. She was doing a commendable job of holding herself together in front of strangers. What she'd do in the privacy of her little trailer was her business.

"Mrs. Sloan, if there's anything I can do, or the department—" Martin Holman had managed to maneuver close enough that he could stand with his back to the grave and still see Miriam Sloan's face.

She looked up slowly and squinted at Holman, her pudgy, florid face wrinkling against the bright sky. "You can find who did this," she said. Then she turned and started back toward the car. I nodded at the deputy, and he and Gayle escorted the woman to the road.

Coroner Emerson Clark had come and gone long since, and there was nothing left but to turn the body over to the patient ambulance attendants.

"What now?" Sheriff Holman asked. He had taken the opportunity to distance himself another couple paces from the grave, taking advantage of a slight breeze.

"We see what the medical examiner can tell us," I said.

"And in the meantime, what about Mrs. Sloan?"

"Bob Torrez and Gayle will take her home. That'll give her about twenty minutes to do some thinking. Then Estelle and I will pay her a visit."

Holman looked over at Estelle and the baby. "You're going to arrest her?"

"Martin, there's no evidence for that yet. We do want to find out why she lied to me about where her son was."

"There might be a logical reason," Holman said.

"There might be. By morning, the M.E. can tell us what killed him, when, how…and where he might have been buried the first time."

Holman made a face. "That's really disgusting. That someone would do that."

I almost chuckled. "Cheer up, Martin."

"Why?"

"It's going to get worse."

"Shit," he muttered, one of the few times I'd heard him cuss. "I wish I knew what to tell the news reporters."

"Tell them that the body of Todd Sloan, age fifteen, was discovered this afternoon in a shallow grave seven point eight miles west of Posadas. And tell them that currently we're investigating possible links between the death of Sloan and the murder of Stuart Torkelson, fifty-four, a prominent Posadas realtor."

Holman managed a rueful grin. "I can figure that much out for myself, Bill. It's the questions they ask afterward that get all over me."

I watched the ambulance attendants trudging back toward the road with the gurney bobbing between them.

"Just tell 'em 'no comment.'"

Holman fell in step with Estelle and me. "Sometimes this job isn't all that great," he said. I shot a quick glance over at Estelle. Ever polite and politic, she was concentrating on where she put her feet.

We reached the road and Holman held up a hand to ward off Linda Rael. "You'll call me?" he asked me, and I nodded.

"We're going to the hospital for a minute, then on out to the trailer park," I said.

"She won't—"

I shook my head. "Deputy Torrez and Gayle will be with her until we get out there. Not to worry."

Martin Holman looked relieved. He turned to face the cameras.

23

Miriam Sloan hadn't been home more than half an hour before Estelle and I arrived at the trailer park. Dr. Francis Guzman had remained at the hospital to keep an eye on Reuben, who was still resting peacefully. He also took charge of Francis Carlos, giving the nursing staff at Posadas General a chance to oh and ah.

Deputy Bob Torrez stepped up to the window of the Blazer as I pulled into Miriam Sloan's yard.

"Now that you're here, I'd really like to take a run out to the wrecking yard where Trujillo works," he said.

"Fine," I said. "What are you hunting?"

"I figure that if Todd Sloan was involved in the farm supply robbery, that's as good a place as any to start hunting for some of the tools that were taken. I got a pretty complete list from Wayne Sanchez."

"All right. And stay close to a radio. We don't know how any of this is going to shape up, Robert. But you're right. The more loose ends we can nail down, the better."

We parked the Blazer and got out. Miriam Sloan didn't greet us at the door this time. Kenny Trujillo did, though. His old Ford pickup, more decrepit by far than Miriam Sloan's worn-out Oldsmobile, was parked under the kitchen window of the trailer.

"Kenny," I said. His eyes were watchful with the built-in distrust of someone who's had a brush or two with the law. "We need to talk with Miriam now, if she's up to it."

"She's inside."

He stood to one side on the porch as Estelle and I entered the trailer. The floor creaked as the flimsy plywood flexed under my weight.

Miriam Sloan came out of a back room. Her eyes were puffy and she had a ball of tissue wadded in one hand.

"Ma'am, we really need to ask you some questions," I said. "I know it's been rough, but the sooner we get this over with, the sooner we can be out of your hair."

She gestured toward the remains of a three-cushion sofa that spanned from the television console to the veneered particle board bookcase that separated living room and dinette. Two of the three shelves were empty except for dust. On the third were two volumes of condensed novels and a blue plastic bowl.

Estelle and I sat on the sofa. Miriam Sloan settled for a metal straight-backed chair near the kitchen counter. Kenny Trujillo got a beer out of the refrigerator and sat on the other side of the counter.

"Mrs. Sloan," I said, "I'm sure you'll do all you can to help us find your son's killer. But I'm going to be honest with you. We're really up against it. That field out there is about as clean of any clues as it's possible to be." I shook my head and watched while Trujillo shook a cigarette out of its pack. He took his time lighting it.

"One thing really puzzles me," I continued. "You told me earlier that Todd had gone to Florida to live with his father." I stopped for a few seconds. Miriam Sloan's knuckles went whiter as she clenched the tissue. She had been holding me in a fixed glare, but now her gaze wavered. She looked down at her hands.

"I thought he had," she said quietly. "At first, that's what he said he was going to do. Him and Kenny, here...they never did get along too well." She glanced over at her boyfriend, a kid young enough to be her son. "I think he was jealous. I don't know. He was all the time saying he was going to leave, and the last few times, he sounded like maybe he meant it."

"And you would have let him?" I asked.

"He was old enough to make up his own mind about things," Miriam replied. "I mean—" she hesitated. "Nothing I could say would change his mind."

Kenny Trujillo snorted and blew out a cloud of smoke. "That's for sure."

I started to say something, but Miriam interrupted me. "He was spending more and more time with that Staples boy. You know him, I'm sure." I did know Richard Staples and was sure he would be on Robert Torrez's short list of suspects. "I think him and Richard were planning to leave. And the last few days, he must have been staying over with Richard Staples, 'cause he certainly wasn't here. That's why I just thought he'd gone to Florida...like he was promising." She dabbed at her nose with the tissue.

"We have reason to believe that Todd may have been involved in a series of burglaries, Mrs. Sloan." She didn't look up and didn't look surprised. "Do you know anything about that?"

"I don't think he'd do that," she said after a long moment of tissue crumpling. "Now I know—" and she held up a hand to fend off an expected protest from me, "that you people have had your complaints with Todd in the past. But he's been trying harder lately. He's been doing better in school. You ask Mr. Archer."

"He has," Kenny agreed.

"Did he ever mention friends of his maybe being involved in break-ins?" Estelle asked. Her quiet voice was apparently so unexpected that Miriam Sloan's head snapped around. She looked long and hard at Estelle.

"Excuse me. This is Detective Estelle Reyes-Guzman," I said.

"I remember you," Miriam said. She didn't pursue the memory.

"Did he mention friends being involved?"

"He didn't talk to me very much," Miriam said. "The only person he ever mentioned was Richard Staples. He spent a lot of time over there."

"You ought to talk to that kid," Kenny Trujillo said. "He's a real little asshole. He worked out at the wreckin' yard with me a time or two, and he don't know his ass from a hole in the ground. Tries to be a big shot, though. Like he knows it all. I told Todd a time or two he had no business truckin' with that kid, but he wouldn't listen. You know how they are." I was amused by Kenny's social commentary. If he kept working at it, he could take a test to be a juvenile counselor, between beers and his own brushes with the law.

"And you don't have any ideas about what kind of trouble Todd might have been in? That would prompt someone to do something like this?"

"He ain't never been in trouble like this before," Kenny Trujillo said. He ground out the cigarette butt. His brow was furrowed in thought. "Seems to me he must have crossed somebody up." He looked at me. "Seems to me that's what had to happen. You got any ideas?"

I shrugged. "Not yet. But we will." I stood up. "We'll keep you posted, Mrs. Sloan. If you think of anything we should know—"

"We'll call. Yes." She didn't get up.

We left the trailer park after making sure that Deputies Paul Encinos and Eddie Mitchell were in the area. Paul parked his patrol car on the county road east of the trailer park, just below the driveway to Anna Hocking's place. From there, he could watch the back of the Sloans' trailer. Eddie Mitchell, no doubt relieved to be away from the hospital, parked his county car in the driveway of the trailer park, conspicuous as hell.

We pulled out on the county road and Estelle said, "Richard Staples?"

"Yes. Do you want to check back at the hospital first?"

She glanced at her watch. "It's still early yet. Let's visit the kid first."

Richard Staples lived with an aunt, Marianna Perna, in the Casa del Sol Apartments behind the high school. It was one of those dark little corners of the village where I seldom went. Posadas had its own village police force—two full-time officers and three part-timers—and my department tried to leave the village alone unless they requested our help.

An eight-foot chain link and barbwire-topped fence separated the back of the high school gymnasium from the apartment complex's parking lot. I parked along the fence, scanning the eight front doors of Casa del Sol.

The building was single-story, looking like a motel. Each unit couldn't have been more than three small rooms. Marianna Perna lived in 104. The number was broken off the blue door, but the paint wasn't quite as faded where the digits had been. A decrepit Ford Festiva was parked directly in front of the door next to a toddler-sized tricycle, a plastic scooter missing the back axle and wheels, and a small-bore dirt bike missing its back wheel, balanced on two cinder blocks under the engine.

The clutter in front of 104 was repeated, in various colors and details, in front of each apartment.

"Great place," I said. I jotted down the license plate number of the Festiva and reached for the door handle of the Blazer. The radio interrupted me.

"Three ten, PCS."

It was Gayle Sedillos.

"Go ahead," I said.

"Three ten, ten nineteen."

"Is this something that can wait a bit, Gayle?" I asked. She wanted me to return to the office. The only person I could think of who might want to see me was Sheriff Martin Holman, and I wasn't in the mood.

"Negative, sir."

"Ten four. We'll be there in about a minute and a half."

Gayle knew how I worked. She knew I didn't like department business blabbed over the airwaves, and so she was as cryptic as she could be on the radio. But her common sense could be trusted. If she said her visitor couldn't wait, that was that.

I backed out of the apartment parking lot. The sheriff's department was eight blocks away, and my estimate was just about right. As we pulled into the lot, only one vehicle was out of place. Herb Torrance's mud-caked Chevrolet one-ton, its fat, dual-wheeled rump projecting six feet beyond the rear of Gayle's Datsun, was parked in the space reserved for the sheriff.

Herb was standing near the front of the truck, leaning on the hood. He saw us and straightened up.

I pulled in beside his truck. Despite the mud and dirt, the Triple Bar T logo was visible on the door panel.

"Reuben's neighbor," I said to Estelle. "Where's he been all this time?"

"Knowing Mr. Torrance, probably minding his own business," Estelle replied.

A week before, I might have believed that.

24

Herb Torrance's voice was deep and slow with a hint of west Texas twang. I extended a hand and his grip was firm. "Herb, I haven't seen you in a while." He wouldn't have changed much if I hadn't seen him in a decade. He was the same lanky, slightly stooped figure, skin pounded to wrinkled brown by sixty years of New Mexico sun and wind.

"It's been a while," he agreed, and touched his right index finger to the brim of his soiled Stetson. "Ma'am," he said.

"This is Detective Estelle Reyes-Guzman, Herb. You probably remember her."

"Well, sure, I remember this young lady. You're old Reuben Fuentes's niece, ain't you? And as I understand it, my neighbor is giving you folks just a little bit of trouble. That's why I wanted to talk with you all."

"Come on inside."

"Oh, this is fine. It won't take long." He leaned against the fender of his truck again and pushed his hat back on the crown of his head in that universal cowpuncher gesture that says, "I'm gonna talk now."

"I just got back to town from a trip over to Animas. Got me a deal going with the breeder service over there. You probably heard of them."

"Yes. You're talking about Porter's Breeder Service. The artifical insemination folks."

"Them's the ones. Anyways, I just got back this morning, and you coulda knocked me down with a feather when I heard about all the ruckus over at Reuben's place. Damn shame about old Torkelson. I've dealt with him a time or two and he didn't seem like the kind of man who'd get crosswise with somebody."

"No, he didn't," I said.

"And then I drove in this afternoon and my gosh if there ain't something else goin' on. I heard you found a kid all dead and buried out there?"

"Yes."

He shook his head at the wonder of it all. "This world ain't the same no more, sheriff."

"It sure as hell isn't."

"Well, what I wanted to run by you was about the old man's dogs. Carla down to the post office told me about Reuben's dogs, and she was figurin' that maybe it was because of them that the old man and Torkelson had the set-to."

"We just don't know, Herb." Carla Champlin's gossip grapevine, whether accurate or not, worked in nearly nuclear proportions.

"Well maybe I can help some. Lookit here." He turned and made a mark in the dirt on the truck's hood. "The old Mexican's pasture kinda fronts on the county road like this." He drew a line down the hood. "Torkelson's property is right across the road here, and he also owns that hump of land right here." He drew a cigar shape that included the limestone ridge at the base of which the dogs—and Todd Sloan—had been buried.

"Now, you come west across that ridge and you're on Triple Bar T land. Well, no, that ain't quite true. It's BLM, but I've got the grazin' lease. And that land goes right up to that new fence they built around Martinez's Tube, way down the road yonder."

"Right," I said. Estelle was watching Herb Torrance rather than the growing map on the truck's hood.

"All right. Now right here is where I set me some bait last week." He drew a little circle in the dirt. "See, we've been gettin' a few winter calves and that's when the coyotes like to come in. They got one of 'em and cut up a cow pretty bad too. So I set me some bait. And I'm thinkin' that them dogs of Reuben's probably got into that stuff."

"They could have," I said. The distance from Reuben's to the bait was short enough, even for three spoiled pets that didn't roam much. "And if the wind was right, the scent of the bait would carry. You weren't using those charged baits that shoot the stuff into the animal's face?"

Torrance shook his head. "No. I do that sometimes in the spring if things get real bad. But this was just laced meat. Hell, the other would have killed 'em on the spot."

"That's what I was thinking. If they really did get into that stuff, it would explain why one of the dogs made it home. She didn't get a big enough dose. The others made it back to the pasture. That's as far as they got."

"I just wanted to swing by and tell you, 'cause it seems to me that that might make a difference. It'd be a shame if old Reuben up and killed Torkelson because he thought the man killed his dogs. It ain't too likely. And if I'd known his dogs would go aroamin' I would have set it a good ways further off."

"I imagine you're right, Herb. But these things happen. We appreciate you coming in. I was going to drive out and have a chat with you, but I hadn't gotten the chance. You saved me a trip. One thing you could do. We sent the dog carcasses to the lab for analysis. If you had the brand name of the stuff you used, it'd help. For comparison. That way, we'd know for sure."

He nodded vigorously. "I got it right here." He walked around me, opened the tool box in the back of the truck, pulled out a small carton, and handed it to me. The label was bright yellow with a big red X through the legs-to-the-sky carcass of a black rat. "Rataway," I read and turned the box over.

The contents were mostly corn meal filler laced with a liberal dose of strychnine and other equally attractive alkaloids. It was one of those products designed for no-nonsense ranch use. If a kid accidentally got into that box, the only antidote would be prayer.

"I didn't know you could even buy stuff like this anymore," I said. A notice on the cover and on each side said, Read Warnings and Instructions for Use Inside. I opened the box and pulled out a small paper, similar to those packed with prescription drugs. I handed the box back to Herb and kept the paper. "This will be all we'll need," I said.

"Probably can't buy it in a regular store," Herb said. "Old Wayne Sanchez keeps some on hand all the time down at the feed store, though."

"Herb, you've been a big help. We appreciate you coming in."

"You bet. Who was the kid that got killed?"

"Todd Sloan."

"Don't know the name. Might recognize the face. What'd he do?"

"We don't know."

"And old Torkelson was mixed up somehow, eh?"

"He had the misfortune of being there, yes. We don't know what his involvement was."

Herb nodded, smart enough to recognize from the tone of my voice that he wasn't going to get any other information. "Well, you got your day cut out for you," he said. He tipped his hat to Estelle for a second time. "Ma'am, nice to see you again."

After he left, I glanced at my watch. "You want to talk with the Staples kid now, or pick up Francis, or go to the hospital to check on Reuben...or all of the above?"

Estelle puffed out her cheeks. I could see she was suffering withdrawal from Francis Carlos. "You gave Francis a key?" she asked.

"Yes, he's got a key to the house."

"They'll be fine, then," she said as if she really didn't believe it. "Let's try to talk with the Staples kid. It'll only take a few minutes and then we can swing by the hospital on the way home. I think Richard Staples is important. I've got a feeling that he's a connection somehow."

"He's got to be."

"For one thing," Estelle added, "Kenny Trujillo and Miriam Sloan were very quick to offer him up as an excuse for Todd's behavior."

Long ago, I'd learned to trust most of Estelle's intuitive leaps. This one made as much sense as any. We drove back to the Casa del Sol.

25

The little car was gone this time. The rest of the litter in front of the apartments was unchanged. "Maybe Ms. Perna had to run some errands," I said.

Estelle looked at her watch again.

"Why don't you stay here. I'll go check," I said. As I walked toward 104, the sounds of a squalling infant floated down from another apartment. Francis Carlos must cry sometimes but it was hard to imagine.

The blue door of the Perna apartment needed more than paint. The wood was split in half a dozen places, with a three-foot-long piece of the jamb molding missing just above the bottom hinge. Where the doorbell had once been was a ragged hole with two stubs of wire taped and pushed back into the wood. "Terrific," I muttered, and knocked on the door.

I knocked four times with no response. Between the third and fourth knocks, I turned to look back toward Estelle. At first it was difficult to see what she was doing through the tinted glass of the truck, but then I realized she was using my binoculars. I kept them in the truck out of habit, hanging them by their strap over the barrel of the shotgun, which was secured with electric locks against the dashboard.

Estelle was looking at something down the apartment complex. I knocked one final time, avoiding the temptation to stare in the direction Estelle was scanning.

Satisfied that either no one was home in 104 or that I was being ignored, I trudged back to the Blazer. By the time I was settled in the seat, she had hung the binoculars back over the shotgun.

"What gives?" I asked. "You bird-watching now?" I gestured at the two ravens that were sitting on a telephone cross-tree at the end of the parking lot.

"You were being watched, sir. Look at the back of the school and count four basement windows."

"What are you talking about?" I squinted and leaned forward. The gymnasium back wall was solid red brick, decorated here and there with graffiti dating back to Ruby's first date with Howard in 1959. In another fifty years, the place would be a historical landmark like the National Park Service's Inscription Rock up north.

The only windows in the wall were a row of six small, rectangular openings that extended below ground level. A small well around each one provided access and drainage.

I looked at the fourth window. "You're kidding," I said. I couldn't tell if the window even had glass, much less see a face. "They're all barred, aren't they?"

I reached for the binoculars and had to monkey with the adjustment before the wall jumped into focus. "You certainly messed these up," I said as I squeezed the tubes together to fit my tired eyes.

Estelle ignored the barb. "I don't think you can see anything when the window is closed," she said. "I saw motion earlier. That's when I looked."

I looked over at her with skepticism. "You saw motion, Estelle?"

"Yes, sir. When the window swings open from the bottom, the line of the window breaks the sharp shadow line created by the well around the window. It was really obvious."

"Right."

"The whole time you were at the doorway, the window was held open. When you turned around to come back to the truck, it closed."

"Must be Quasimodo," I said. "One of the janitors is poking around. Either that or you're imagining things."

"A janitor down in the back of the basement, behind the boilers? During Christmas recess?"

"Maybe the janitors work during vacations. I don't know what's down there. And I didn't know you spent your early years down there, either."

Estelle smiled. "I didn't. But I do remember that the locker rooms and all the offices in that building are at the west end...this end. And that means all the plumbing. The only things at the other end are the foyer, the concession stand, and all the trophy cases."

I turned in my seat and looked hard at Estelle. I squinted my eyes, trying to see into her brain. She grinned and shrugged. "Sorry. I saw it."

"Are you sure?"

"*Claro.*"

"This is ridiculous," I said and started the Blazer. I backed out onto the street, drove a quarter block and turned into the high school's circular driveway. "If we don't check, neither one of us will get any sleep," I said.

Estelle grinned. "When did you start sleeping, sir?"

"Heh, heh."

I parked next to a late model Caravan with a bumper sticker on the back that read MY SON IS AN HONOR STUDENT AT POSADAS MIDDLE SCHOOL. It was the only vehicle in the lot, parked in the slot nearest the cafeteria wing between the gymnasium and the office.

"Let's save some steps," I said and picked up the mike. I called in the license plate of the van, and in four minutes we knew that it was registered to Elwood Kessel. Kessel was one of the assistant football and basketball coaches. He taught science and civics on occasion. Not surprisingly, no one had filed a want or warrant for him through the National Crime Information Center.

I reached down and slid my heavy flashlight out from under the seat. "You might want to grab the one in the glove box. Basements are dark places, assuming we get in. The door to the coaches' office is over on the west side of the gym," I said. "Best bet." And it was. We rounded the corner of the gym just as Kessel was in the process of turning the deadbolt behind him.

"Jesus, you startled me," he said. He pulled his key out of the lock and shook the handle. He was young, twenty times fitter than I ever was, with brown hair that he probably had to work on for an hour to make it look so casually unruly. "Who can I help you find?" He might have found it odd to meet two people holding flashlights in the bright sunshine of afternoon.

"Well, you, for starters," I said. And even though I said it as casually as I could, I saw the flicker of uneasiness that most civilians feel when they have to talk with uniforms. I introduced us, although that was hardly necessary since my name tag on the uniform shirt was clearly visible, and Kessel's eyes had strayed there first.

"What can I do for you?"

"Is there any one else in the building besides yourself, coach?"

He had thrust his hands in the back pockets of his jeans and he leaned forward as if he hadn't heard my question. "Excuse me?"

"Is there any one else in the building?"

"No sir. Not that I know of. There shouldn't be. Why?"

"Are this and the front door the only two means of entry?"

The coach frowned. "What's this all about, anyway?"

"We're not sure. Probably nothing. But it would help if you'd answer my question."

He blushed. "Sure. There's another door on the east side. It exits out of the back of the snack bar."

"That's it? The three doors?"

"Yes."

"Were you downstairs just a few minutes ago?"

"Downstairs? No. Why would I go downstairs?" He tried for a chuckle. "The boiler is the janitor's problem, not mine. But they all went home at four."

I moved toward the door. It was heavy steel. "Would you mind?"

He hesitated. "Uh—"

"Coach Kessel, we're not executing a warrant or anything like that. Let me tell you what happened." I put a hand on his shoulder, father to son. "Detective Reyes-Guzman and I were in the parking lot of the Casa Del Sol apartments just now." I waved a hand. "Other business. She said she saw one of the basement windows open. Someone was looking out."

Kessel turned and looked at Estelle. He couldn't think of anything to say, so he shrugged and held out his hands, palms up.

"We'd like to take a look. And I'll be honest with you. We've got a couple reasons other than being concerned that someone's in your building after hours. But I really don't want to go into that now."

I took my hand off his shoulder and put it on the door handle. "Would you?"

"Sure." He pulled the wad of keys out of his pocket and unlocked the door. The effluvia was instantaneous, even though the nearest locker room was fifty feet down a hallway and through two more doors. Maybe coaches got used to the continuous smell of socks, uniforms, mildewed towels, and decaying sneakers. "Through here," he said and I started to follow him. Then I remembered the person behind me.

"You want to stay with the truck? In case someone needs to reach us on the radio?"

"No." Estelle had the courtesy not to tack "foolish old man" to the end of her remark.

I nodded. We wound through first the boys' locker room and then the girls'; neither was a pretty sight. I wondered what microbiologists would find if they took cultures of the things growing on the shower stall walls.

"Right here," Kessel said. "This is one of two doors downstairs." He hesitated. "At least I think there's two. Obviously I don't go down there much." He didn't look like he wanted to go down this time, either.

He snapped on the light switch to illuminate the concrete stairway. I could hear a steady humming and presumed it came from the snarl of wires and transformers that began at the foot of the stairs and continued along the wall for a dozen feet. Light streamed in through a twenty-four-inch-wide window that was heavily barred.

"This is the west corner?" I said, keeping my voice low.

"I guess," Kessel said.

"So this is the sixth window," I said for Estelle's benefit. She nodded, looking off into the musty darkness behind the boiler with what seemed to me idle curiosity.

I squeezed past what might have been a fuel oil tank and the first boiler. I nodded at the steel door that faced me.

"I don't know," Kessel said. The door was locked. "Maybe my master key fits," he said without much enthusiasm. It did, and the door yawned inward. A question that had kept me awake for many nights was answered as the door opened and the lights were switched on. The room was filled with hundreds of old desks... hundreds. They were stacked neatly to the ceiling girders, their legs interlocked like strange, metallic spiders.

"So this is where they go," I whispered. I looked at Kessel, who was plainly nervous. "Old desks...you gotta wonder," I said.

"And that's number four," Estelle said. We made our way down an aisle between Type A-2 desks from the fifties and a collection of rare C-24s from the early sixties...the kind with the folding writing wing that hits you squarely in the shins, every time.

Sure enough, the window wasn't latched. Estelle reached up and pushed it open. It swung on hinges from the top, and its travel was limited to about six inches.

"Well, well," I said. The lights from the overheads didn't reach the musty corners and I turned on my flashlight. "Hold still a second," I said, and Estelle froze near the wall. Coach Kessel didn't need to be told. I bent down with a grunt.

"What is it?"

"A nacho chip," I said, holding up the yellow corn chip. I sniffed it and snapped off a corner. "Fresh." I looked at Estelle. "Congratulations, sharp eyes."

I swept my flashlight around the room. The next door heading eastward was padlocked. "What's in there?"

"I don't know," Kessel said.

"My guess would be the main electrical service," Estelle said. "That's about where the wires hit the building on the outside."

I swept my light around the room, probing. "So if someone was down here, they'd have to leave the way we came in," I said. "Unless there's another hallway or something. Which there might well be." I was making my way up the aisle with my pulse hammering in my ears. The corner of my flashlight beam had found itself a tennis shoe...just the toe at first.

But as the light touched it, the shoe moved ever so slightly, drawing back like an earthworm from the fisherman's flashlight. "Someone would have to have a hell of a lot of keys to turn this place into a hotel," I said, keeping my light away from the shoe.

During some other epoch, several dozen desks had lost their grip and tumbled into a welter of chrome and imitation oak plywood. It created a perfect warren, home to the sneakers and the legs attached to them. With my right hand resting loosely on the butt of my service revolver I swept the light quickly to the left, stabbing the beam full into the cowering youngster's face.

"Hello, Richard," I said.

26

"I didn't do nothin'," Richard Staples said immediately...the expected litany of the teenager who's guilty as hell.

"Stand up, son," I said. "And keep your hands where I can see them."

He did so, unwinding with some care so that none of the desk mountains were dislodged. "I didn't do nothin'," he repeated, and I knew that we weren't dealing with a rocket scientist. I left my flashlight on, even though there was plenty of light now that Staples wasn't hiding under the furniture.

He was taller than I was by half a foot and husky to boot. If he decided to make a bulldozer run for the door behind me, I'd be hard-pressed to stop him. "Put your hands on top of your head," I snapped. "Right now."

He looked over toward Estelle and Kessel as if to see if they were allies or obstacles. In his best, most reasonable coach's voice, Elwood Kessel said, "Don't make it hard on yourself, son. Do what the officer says."

As Staples's hands drifted up toward his head, I pushed my advantage. "Now turn around." Estelle maneuvered through the desks and took my handcuffs out of the belt keeper. In one deft motion she snapped them first on his right wrist, yanked his arm down and around, and then followed with his left.

Different people react in different ways to custody. I'd had grown men piss their pants and grovel when the cuffs clicked, and I'd had elderly women turn into kicking banshees...and every combination in between. Richard Staples turned and glowered first at Estelle and then me.

"I didn't do nothin'," he said. His round, acne-pocked face was defiant. He hunched his shoulders, trying the strength of the handcuffs.

"What were you doing down here?"

"None of your business." He turned to look at Kessel and sneered, the twisted lip making his unattractive face none the better. "There ain't nothin' wrong with bein' here."

"Is that a fact," I said. "Trespass is still a crime in New Mexico, as far as I know."

"I wasn't trespassin'. This is a school."

The logic of that escaped me. I took hold of his right arm just above the elbow and exerted some pressure toward the door. "We can talk down at the office."

"You ain't got no right to do this," Staples said and I heard a faint, plaintive quality for the first time.

"You have the right to shut your mouth, son. I don't know what game you're playing, but it won't take long to find out. Estelle, would you go on ahead and call in? Tell whoever is on dispatch that I want Deputy Torrez to meet us at the side door of the gym, ASAP." She nodded and vanished through the desks toward the boiler room.

I crouched down and swept the flashlight beam around the room, bouncing it off half a million chrome legs. Wherever the kid kept his stash, it wasn't there.

Richard Staples didn't say anything else until we were halfway through the first locker room upstairs. "I ain't done nothin' wrong," he said to whoever would listen. I paid no attention.

"Coach, will you do me a favor? Call Glenn Archer and have him meet us down at the sheriff's office?"

"You want me to do that right now?"

"Right now," I said. We reached the coaches' office and Kessel made for the phone. The door to the parking lot opened and Estelle looked inside.

"Torrez will be here in about two minutes, sir."

"Fine. Son, have a seat." I pointed at one of the straightbacked chairs. Staples did so, with a expression that said he'd tear me limb from limb if I'd oblige by taking off the handcuffs. He sat on the edge of the chair as if he were painfully constipated.

"Mrs. Archer?" Kessel said into the telephone. "This is Elwood Kessel down at the school. Is Mr. Archer there?" He waited and I could hear the shrill chatter of Dorothy Archer's voice across the room. "Well, we've got a little problem down at the school, and I need to reach him." Again the chatter, and I waved a hand, gesturing for the receiver.

"Mrs. Archer? This is Undersheriff Bill Gastner. Where can we reach your husband?"

"Well, as I was telling Coach Kessel, Glenn said he was going downtown to buy a new pair of shoes. My goodness, what's going on?"

"Nothing earthshaking. We just need to see him. The sooner the better. Could you do us a favor, ma'am?"

"What's that?"

"Would you track him down for us? Tell him I need to speak with him at the sheriff's office?"

"Well, I...I'll certainly do my best."

"Thank you, ma'am." I handed the telephone back to Kessel.

"How'd he get in here?" Kessel asked. Staples ignored him.

"That's one reason he's in cuffs," I said. "I would imagine we'll find some interesting things in his pockets."

"You ain't going to search nothin'," Staples said with venom.

"That's the other reason you're in cuffs, son."

"Yeah, well—"

Estelle stepped outside and I saw her wave an arm.

"Let's go," I said and Staples gave me that wonderful sneer that said "*You old fat fart, if you'd take these off...*"

I didn't bother to argue. I waited about ten seconds, long enough for a car door to slam and footsteps to reach the entrance to the coaches' office. Deputy Bob Torrez appeared in the doorway. He filled most of it.

"What's this?" he said, looking down from his six feet four at the seated youth.

"This is Richard Staples. He's taking a ride with you downtown." Posadas didn't have a downtown, but it sounded good. "Read him his rights and book him on criminal trespass and unlawful entry."

"All right. Let's go." He crooked an index finger in Staples's direction. The kid hesitated just long enough and then pushed to his feet.

"I didn't do nothin'," he said. I knew his attitude wasn't going to change as long as he had an audience and until we were able to tie some pieces together. For the moment, I was content just to have him under lock and key.

"We'll be down in a minute, Robert," I said. "Glenn Archer is going to meet us there. Make sure that kid isn't out of cuffs for even a second. If he has to go to the bathroom, tell him to piss his pants."

Staples looked pained at that, but he quickly recovered. Torrez deposited him in the back seat of the county car, behind the heavy screen. When a kid landed there for the first time, he usually mellowed a bit when he saw there were no door handles, no window cranks, no door locks. It's the first small taste of jail. But Staples didn't bat an eye.

"What do you think, sir?" Estelle said as we watched the county car drive out of the lot.

"I think he's glad we've got him," I said.

"I was thinking the same thing," Estelle Reyes-Guzman said. "He wasn't hiding in the basement of the school just to avoid us."

"Even if he saw us and was tipped off when we first pulled into the apartment parking lot, he wouldn't have done that," I said. "He could have just ignored my knock on the door."

"He didn't look very overjoyed to me," Elwood Kessel said.

"It's easy to be brave when you know how you're going to be treated," I said. "He may be in cuffs, but he's safe with us…he can practice being a hardass without worrying about getting the shit kicked out of him." I stuck out my hand. "You were a great help," I said.

Kessel looked puzzled as he shook my hand. I was puzzled too, but I tried not to look it.

27

I wanted Richard Staples to stew a little bit, so I suggested that Estelle and I swing by the hospital.

Reuben Fuentes was sleeping peacefully. Estelle flipped a page on his chart and frowned at all the numbers.

"They checked his BP and pulse just half an hour ago."

"How's he doing?"

"I don't know. I wish I could read it." She looked heavenward. "Doctors." She slipped the clipboard back in its bracket and moved around to the table near the head of the bed. She picked up a folded piece of yellow paper and glanced at the message. "Francis took the baby home," she said.

"Home?" I asked, feeling a twinge of panic.

"Your house," she said, and smiled. "We need to stop by there for a few minutes." She rested her palm on Reuben's wrinkled forehead for a moment. The old man didn't stir, but his breathing was regular and easy. Estelle took his pulse at the wrist. "Eighty-eight," she said. "That doesn't seem too bad to me."

"He must be doing better. They took him off drip," I said, remembering the relief I'd felt when they'd jerked the damn needles out of me. When we were out in the hallway, headed for the car, I asked, "What are your plans?"

She took a deep breath. "I don't know. I want to talk with Francis for a few minutes to see what he found out today. I guess we'll play it from there."

"You know," I said, "that even if your great-uncle does recover, he may need constant care."

Estelle grimaced. "He's going to hate that more than anything else in the world, sir."

"A fact of life, though."

"I'll wait and see what Francis says," Estelle said.

"He's in the clear now as far as this case goes, though." I held the outside door open for her. "You certainly don't have to go dragging around with me, investigating a case that doesn't have anything to do with Reuben. He couldn't have killed the boy or Torkelson."

Estelle looked at me and raised an eyebrow. "You're sending us home?"

"Come on. You're welcome to stay as long as you like. Both of you...all three of you. More than welcome. What I'm saying is that you have better things to do than chase around the countryside on a busman's holiday."

"We'll see what Francis has to say."

I unlocked the Blazer. "You're sounding positively domestic, Estelle."

"That can't be all bad."

I didn't bother to check in with the office when we left the hospital, but drove straight home. Francis was stretched out on the old leather sofa in the den, shoes off, head propped up on two pillows, the television on, and little Francis Carlos curled up on his stomach like an awkward, hairless puppy.

I glanced at the television. Lauren Bacall was bristling at the Duke's refusal to take his meals downstairs with the other boarders.

"This is a pretty good movie," Francis said, careful not to shift his position.

"It's the only one I've got." I watched for a few seconds. "I don't think I've ever seen this part. I always fall asleep."

Francis picked up the remote and popped the set off. "Estelle, you want to take *chiquito-ito-ito* here for a minute so I can get up?" Estelle took the baby, who blinked in surprise and then looked at me over his mother's shoulder. He frowned.

"What's the latest?" Francis asked, swinging his feet off the couch.

"That's what we came to ask you," Estelle said. "I looked at Uncle Reuben's chart, but I couldn't read it. He was sleeping when we left."

"Actually, he's doing really well, considering." Francis ran a hand through his thick black hair. "I'm amazed. He was awake when I checked in on him about two hours ago. He asked if you two were out at the cabin. He wanted to know if the place was all right. I said it was, and that you'd be in later with a report. He was relieved that someone hadn't walked off with the ranch." Francis paused and laced his fingers together.

"The problem, of course, is that we've got a patient who's ninety years old or so with congestive heart failure. And that's apt to bring on all kinds of other complications. There are already some signs of kidney failure, pulmonary edema…on and on. One thing just sort of leads to another."

"All this just comes on suddenly?" Estelle asked. She sat down on one of the hassocks with the kid in her lap.

"Of course not. But my theory is that with someone like Reuben, his pattern of living just slows down to compensate. He accomplishes in a day what you or I would do in fifteen minutes. And he can continue doing that, functioning slower and slower, until something comes along to upset the applecart." Francis held up his hands. "The flu or pneumonia…a broken hip, a stroke."

"In this case, finding his pets dead and then deciding that he has to bury them himself," I said.

"Sure." Francis nodded.

"So what's best? Is he going to need extended nursing care?" Francis took a deep breath and glanced over at me. "No."

"Then what?"

"Estelle, Reuben and I talked about more than just his cabin this afternoon. He's really pretty aware of what's going on, and what his prospects are. He's refused any more medication of any kind."

"Is that why he was taken off the drip?"

"Yes. As far as I'm concerned, and as far as Dr. Perrone is concerned, he was lucid when he made the decision and request."

"He'll just sink, won't he?"

"Yes."

Estelle lowered her head so that her chin rested lightly on top of the baby's head. She blew out a long breath that mussed his fine, black hair. "Any happy news?" she said, breaking the silence.

"The position is mine if I want it," Francis replied.

Estelle looked at me sideways without moving her head from the baby's. The crow's-feet at the corners of her eyes deepened.

"What position is yours if you want it?" I asked, already knowing the answer. There was nothing about Reuben's condition that would warrant all the meetings with first Perrone and then Fred Tierney, the hospital administrator.

"Allen Perrone wants to expand his practice in this part of the state. He wants more of a clinic approach, with four or five of us under the same roof so patients don't have to travel."

"Of *us*," I said.

"Right. He wrote me to pop the idea a month or so ago, after a convention in Albuquerque. I mentioned to him then that we were thinking of relocating back down here to make school easier for Estelle."

I turned my head slowly and fixed Estelle with a blank stare. "School? Why am I the last person to know all this?"

"I was going to surprise you next week, at the christening."

My smile kept spreading wider and wider until I felt downright silly. "Well—" I started, and was interrupted by the telephone in the kitchen. "Let me get this and then—" I glanced at my watch. Bob Torrez had had almost an hour to package Richard Staples up and send him upstairs to one of the cozy eight-by-tens.

"Gastner."

Bob Torrez's voice was slow and deliberate. "Sir, are you going to be able to come down to the office before long?"

"What's up?"

"Glenn Archer is here. He isn't too happy."

"He's never happy," I said. "Tell him I'll be down there in about six minutes."

"And Mrs. Perna is here. She's not too happy either."

"Wonderful."

"And Linda Rael wants to talk to you."

"I'll bet she does. I don't want to talk to her. Is that all?"

"So far, sir."

"I'll be right there. Is Sheriff Holman in the office?"

"Yes, sir. He's standing between Glenn Archer and Mrs. Perna at the moment."

"Take a picture for me." I hung up. When I walked back into the den, I saw Dr. Francis Guzman sitting on the couch with the infant in his lap. "Where's Estelle?"

Francis put on his most patient face. "She's waiting at the front door, sir."

"For God's sake," I said and stomped out of the room. It was going to take all my willpower to wipe the grin off my face by the time I got to the office.

28

I knew I had precious little time for mental celebration...maybe the six minutes it would take to drive to the sheriff's office. Estelle rarely volunteered information, even to me—hell, maybe not even to Francis. I had gotten used to asking questions, whether the topic was any of my business or not.

"What are you going to study?"

"I'd like to eventually get into law," she said.

I almost swerved into the big cottonwood whose roots were heaving Fernando Stewart's sidewalk up out of the ground at the end of Guadalupe Lane.

"Law? You mean like in lawyers?"

"Right."

"Christ, Estelle. You don't read much Shakespeare, do you." She smiled. "Well," I added, "I guess there's always room for a good one, and you'll be a good one, gal."

"I hope so."

"Where are you going to school?"

"I'm going to start at Cruces in the fall." She grimaced. "It'll take three years or so to get my bachelor's. That'll give me time to decide if this is really something I want to do."

"And then? After law school? Where are you going to make your millions? Wall Street?"

"Sure. I can see me in New York City, sir."

"You'll do fine anywhere. For selfish reasons, I can always hope you guys end up out here."

"We'll be here for a while," she said. "One step at a time."

I pulled into the parking lot of the sheriff's office and cursed. Someone's green Mitsubishi was in my parking spot. The sheriff's Buick was carefully parked so that it took up not only Holman's spot but half of another. All of the other spaces were taken as well.

"Don't these people have anything goddamned better to do?" I muttered, and parked directly in front of the gasoline pumps.

As we got out of the truck and walked toward the building, Estelle hooked her hand through my elbow for ten paces and gave my arm an affectionate squeeze. "Take a deep breath and count to fifty, sir," she said.

We walked through the door and instantly I wanted to be back home, snuggled in my warm, quiet den watching the second two-thirds of my one movie. Martin Holman stood in the short hallway that led to the dispatcher's office. He was leaning with one elbow on top of the filing cabinet, the other hand hooked in his belt. His back was to the door.

Facing him, broad of beam and steel gray hair tied up in a tight, determined bun, was Marianna Perna. She was talking and Holman was listening, nodding in rhythm as if he was directing a band in two-two time. I didn't know Mrs. Perna well, but had crossed tracks with her a time or two in the village offices where she worked as one of the billing clerks.

She was wagging her index finger under Holman's nose, and I wondered how long she'd had him pegged there. Eight steps beyond Mrs. Perna and her hostage stood Robert Torrez. At first glance it looked as if he had wadded up and crumpled Glenn Archer into a corner, but I realized the high school principal was sitting on the edge of the small reports table, his arms folded across his chest. What surprised me most was that he was listening...and Deputy Torrez was talking.

Standing half in and half out of the dispatch room, which meant the rest of her was in my office, was Linda Rael. She had to be talking with someone interesting, since she wasn't haunting either Holman or Archer.

Holman turned at the sound of the storm door slamming and relief flooded his face.

I nodded at Mrs. Perna, making sure my own expression was set in stone.

"Ma'am, I'll need to talk with you in a bit," I said before she had a chance to launch an attack at her new target. "Sheriff, can I have a minute? Let's use my office." I continued past them and beckoned to Glenn Archer. He wasn't a happy camper, but he followed me without question.

"Bob, make sure Mrs. Perna stays close," I said as I walked past the deputy. He nodded, but I was already headed for Linda Rael. She turned, saw me, and raised both eyebrows as if to say, "*Ah, here's the scoop.*"

"Ms. Rael, you'll have to excuse us for a few minutes," I said. Sitting on the edge of my desk, looking as unperturbed as only a lawyer can, was Ron Schroeder, the district attorney we shared with two other rural counties who couldn't afford their own.

I breathed a sigh of relief. I liked Schroeder. He worked hard, was a good listener, and didn't make too many mistakes. Some of his plea bargain deals left me a little cold, but I knew the pressures on his office from district court.

"Bill, how you doin'" Schroeder said, pushing himself away from the desk. We shook hands.

"Ron, you know Glenn Archer, don't you? Principal at the high school."

"Of course. Glenn, good to see you."

Holman started to close the door in Estelle's face and I said, maybe just a shade too sharply, "I need the detective in on this, sheriff." Holman looked at me, frowned, shrugged, then held the door for Estelle.

"I'm glad you showed up," Holman said. He latched the door and leaned against it. The subconscious action wasn't lost on me...Marianna Perna was on the other side, and she was pissed.

"How long have you been holding the kid?" Schroeder asked. He hooked one of the straight chairs over and sat down, leaning it back against the wall.

"We took him into custody at about two minutes after five," I said. "Glenn, as the deputy no doubt told you, Richard Staples was arrested in the basement storage room under the gymnasium."

"The deputy didn't tell me much," Archer said. He rubbed a hand across his bald head.

"I'm telling you now," I said as pleasantly as I could. Archer always reminded me of the mousey little guys who played accountants for the mob in grade B movies. He'd been principal for eleven years, something of an accomplishment in Posadas...and he'd proven himself a bright, innovative educator.

"It appeared that Staples was hiding in the basement for protection. He was uncooperative when we found him."

"That place is locked in a dozen places," Archer said. "How'd he get in?"

I looked across at Estelle. "Would you go ask Deputy Torrez if he has had time to conduct a personal inventory search of Staples, and if he has, would you bring the envelope?"

She slipped out, closing the door quietly behind herself. I continued, "There was no sign of forced entry. The way that building is put together, there's only one answer that's plausible. Now, the reason I needed to meet with all of you gentlemen is a little sticky." I stopped as the door opened. Estelle had a manila envelope in hand.

I took it and walked around behind my desk. The contents were lean—one thin wallet, three dimes, a nickel, seven pennies, a Buck pocket knife, and a key ring with six keys. I picked up the key ring.

"Best?" I said, glancing up at Archer. "The school keys are Best?"

He fumbled in his pocket and pulled out a jangling wad. "Yes," he said, "and key shops won't duplicate them, either."

I held out Staples's key ring to Archer. He took it and grunted. "How the hell did he get his hands on a double A master?"

"Maybe he'll tell us that. What will that key open?"

"Anything on the west end of the campus, from the gymnasium to the kitchen. Even the little storage building behind the kitchen."

"Any of the office space?"

Archer shook his head. "That's another key series. But Staples could walk into the gymnasium any time he wanted. Weight room, furnace room, anywhere except the concession storage. That's a padlock. The Boosters' Club and I have a key to that."

"So he had himself his own private hangout after hours," Holman said. "But he didn't take anything?"

Archer looked pained. "Who knows what we'll find out when we really start looking, sheriff. You know how it is. A teacher reports this or that missing and what can we do? We don't strip search the entire school. We tell the teachers not to leave money lying around, and lock up equipment when it's not in use. But, like I said…who knows what we'll find."

I held up a hand. "We don't have a whole lot of time until the sheriff, the district attorney, and I have to deal with young mister Staples's guardian, so let me lay the cards out for you." I sat down behind my desk.

"Estelle and I have good cause to believe that Richard Staples is somehow involved with the murders of Todd Sloan and Stuart Torkelson. I'm sure you've heard by the grapevine what's been going on this weekend."

"You've got to be kidding," Glenn Archer said.

"No, I'm not kidding. We don't have any solid connection yet, but I have a couple reasons to believe there's an association. First—" I hesitated and looked at Archer. He was listening carefully. "Glenn, you can appreciate the confidentiality of this. Nothing we talk about in here can leave this room."

"Of course." He looked pained that I had had to say it.

"Good. First, Estelle and I interviewed Todd Sloan's mother and her live-in boyfriend, Kenny Trujillo, after she identified the boy's remains. They both indicated that Todd had been hanging around with Richard Staples a lot recently."

Archer frowned, but said nothing.

"They said that if Todd Sloan had been involved in any of the break-ins we've had recently, that it might be because of that association with Richard." I shrugged. "Maybe, maybe not. But that establishes some kind of connection between the two, however tenuous. In a community this small, it's only logical to expect that Richard would know something about Todd's murder, even if he had no hand in committing it. Everyone follow?" I looked around the room.

"And second?" Archer asked.

"Second is even less substantial," I said. "It was clear to both Detective Reyes-Guzman and me that Richard Staples was hiding when we found him…he sure as hell wasn't having much of a party down there in the dark with all those antique desks. But he wasn't hiding from us. At least I don't think so."

"What makes you sure?" Holman asked.

"For one thing, he didn't have any real warning that we were coming. We did pull into the apartment parking lot about fifteen minutes before, but we then left without going in. We returned, as I said, in about fifteen minutes, but Staples wouldn't have known we were coming back." I leaned back in my chair and took a deep breath.

"And even if he did know, he had no reason to hide. We were driving my civilian vehicle. When I went to his apartment to knock, there was nothing threatening in my bearing. I was in uniform, so he would have known who I was. Estelle remained in the vehicle. He could have just ignored us. He could have ignored my knock. Even an idiot would know that an old fat man isn't going to break down the door."

Ron Schroeder was the only one who smiled at that.

"I know it's tenuous, but there are enough tidbits to warrant a good long talk with Mr. Staples. And that's where I need some help."

"Help?" Archer asked.

"Yes. No one throws a kid in jail for hiding in the basement of a school, especially if he used a key to gain entry and didn't commit any vandalism or theft. He was just there, hiding like a scared rabbit."

"I can understand that."

"We need to establish what he knows, and that may take some time, it may take some threats, it may take some sweet talk. I don't know this kid yet."

"I can tell you a little about him," Archer said. "He was suspended for truancy in November."

"Suspended for truancy?" I said. "That's an interesting concept."

Archer was in no mood to discuss educational psychology. "He's eighteen years old, and has enough credits to be a high school freshman."

"You don't need any credits to be a freshman, do you?" Holman asked.

"That's the point," the principal said. "Richard Staples attends school for the social and vocational benefits, not for anything else. And by vocational, I mean he's a hell of a talented salesman. Whether the material he sells belongs to him is of little concern. But one thing surprises me in what you say, Mr. Gastner." Archer rearranged himself on the chair.

"I've known both boys most of their lives. Todd Sloan was showing some signs, however small, of coming around. He's in trouble a lot—I should say *was* in trouble a lot—for little things. But in the past semester he really showed some signs of trying. He was, what, fifteen? Maybe sixteen? That means he was two grade levels behind his age group. But this past semester he made the merit list. That doesn't mean he had tremendous grades, necessarily. What it does mean is that at least three teachers singled him out as making commendable progress in some fashion." Archer shrugged. "So, he was trying a little."

"Did he hang around with Staples in school?" Schroeder asked.

"That's what surprises me about all this. No, he didn't. In fact, both boys were involved really early in the year in a fight of some kind. Sloan was a scrappy little kid. He got into trouble at the middle school for fighting all the time." Archer shook his head. "I never saw the two together, except that one incident. I think it was in September. It was a ruckus in phys ed class and involved three or four other youngsters as well."

"So if they were working together after hours, they kept the fact well disguised," I said.

"Right."

"Here's the problem, then. We have no real reason to keep Staples in custody. Yeah, technically, he committed a couple of crimes by being in the school. But he caused no damage that we're aware of, and no harm to another person."

Archer nodded. Ron Schroeder leaned forward. "What Bill needs, Glenn, is for you to sign a formal complaint against Richard Staples. That way, he's got cause to hold the young man until a preliminary arraignment with the magistrate. Granted, that will only take a few hours, or even less...but it might give these folks enough time to make some connections."

The idea clearly made Glenn Archer uncomfortable. "And if I don't? I mean, as you say, there isn't much cause."

"Well, that's not really true," the district attorney said. "We can hold him for questioning, especially since we're investigating two capital crimes, and there is some probable cause to believe Staples is involved, however tangentially. It's just that with a formal, signed complaint from you, any problems down the road are ruled out."

"And think of it this way, Glenn," I said. "If we're right, and Richard Staples was hiding from someone else, his being in our custody might well keep him alive."

Archer nodded. "Let's find out what's going on."

29

Marianna Perna was one cheerleader who wasn't in our corner. As far as she was concerned, little Dicky Staples could do no wrong, which explained for me why the kid was in the fix he was.

"Now I want to know what you people think you're doing," she said, and her body English, massive in itself, told me she was going to block the hallway until she got an answer.

Sheriff Martin Holman started to hem and haw and I stepped forward to fix Mrs. Perna with my best Marine Corps gunnery sergeant's glare. "We know exactly what we're doing, Mrs. Perna. Let me explain something to you." It wasn't lost on either of us that Linda Rael was standing quietly in the corner behind Deputy Tony Abeyta, who was taking a turn at dispatch. Linda was holding a small tape recorder.

"We're up to here," and I tapped one of the wattles under my chin, "in a murder investigation…a double homicide. We have reliable information that Richard Staples may be aware of some evidence critical to this investigation. And I'll repeat that for you…*may be aware.*"

She started to squawk and I held up a hand and frowned. "We also have information that Richard Staples may be involved in some way with at least one residential burglary."

"Now I want to know—" Mrs. Perna began.

"First you need to listen, Mrs. Perna. Detective Reyes-Guzman and I visited your apartment today in order to talk with Richard Staples. Our intent was to seek information only. He could have opened the door, chatted with me for five minutes, and that might have been that. But he chose not to do that. For whatever reason, Richard Staples illegally entered the high school gymnasium, using a master key that he had in his possession." Mrs. Perna looked more puzzled than brazen when she heard that.

"As an employee of the village, you know full well that a master key in the wrong hands is a problem indeed. Young Staples has no business with that key. The conclusion I would reach is one of two: Either he stole the key from someone, or the key was given to him by someone who in turn stole it. It really doesn't matter at the moment. At any rate, Richard Staples entered the school and was observed by a law enforcement officer looking out of one of the windows.

"We apprehended him in the basement of the school and took him into custody. That, ma'am, is what is going on."

Mrs. Perna counted to ten and switched targets from us to Richard Staples. "I want to talk with that young man. I'll find out what he thinks he's doing."

She turned and looked down the hall as if that were the direction of the holding pen.

"No, ma'am, you may not talk with Mr. Staples. He is in our custody and will remain so until his preliminary arraignment this evening before Justice Emilio Gutierrez."

"I have a right to talk with my nephew, and I want to talk with him right now."

I looked at Mrs. Perna with considerable exasperation, tinged with just a little admiration.

"Sorry, Mrs. Perna. Number one, and you can check with the district attorney if you feel I'm wrong, you don't have any right to see your nephew just now. He's no longer a minor and he's under arrest." I glanced at my watch. "We're due at arraignment at six-fifteen. That's an hour and a half from now. If you would like to wait, you'll have a chance to see Richard for a few moments while he's being transported to Justice Gutierrez's. Beyond that, you'll just have to be patient. And now, if you'll excuse me, we have a great deal to do." I gestured at the two vinyl-covered chairs between the file cabinets. "You're welcome to wait there if you like."

Mrs. Perna looked at me and then at Sheriff Holman, who hadn't said squat during the entire exchange.

Holman nodded and frowned. "You're welcome to wait out here," he said. "Excuse us."

I turned and beckoned Deputy Torrez and Estelle Reyes-Guzman to follow.

The stairway up to the cells was steep, the wood deeply cupped in spots from decades of traffic. On one side of the upstairs hallway were six small, dismal jail cells. About all that could be said for them was that they were secure. In twenty-three years, I could remember no time when all six had been full.

Across the hall were a storage room, a photographic dark room, and the conference room. District Attorney Ron Schroeder, with other fish to fry who probably paid fifty bucks an hour, begged off.

"Lemme know what you need, Bill," he said. "I'll be in my office."

"And miss all the fun?" I asked.

"Such fun," he said. "I'll pass."

Deputy Torrez went down to cell six and after much clanking and door-slamming returned with a somber Richard Staples. I pointed to the straight ladder-backed chair on one side of the oak table.

"Sit there, Richard," I said. Torrez escorted him to his seat and then joined Estelle and me opposite Staples. After considerable obvious indecision, Sheriff Holman sat at the end of the table, like father at dinner.

I gestured at the tape recorder in the center of the table.

"This interview is being recorded," I said as I punched the two buttons down. "Has Deputy Torrez advised you of your rights?"

"Yes."

"You'll have to speak louder, Richard."

"Yes, he advised me," Staples said and I saw the VU meter on the recorder jump. His former bravado had evaporated. An hour in the dungeon had been the right medicine.

"Richard, I want to make sure you know all the people present." I pointed at each person in turn. "On my left is Deputy Robert Torrez. This is Deputy Estelle Reyes-Guzman from the Isidro County sheriff's department." I saw a flicker in Staples's expression. Maybe he was wondering what the hell he'd done up north to pull the cops down on him from there. Maybe he was too stupid to know where Isidro County was.

"And this is Sheriff Martin Holman. I'm Undersheriff William Gastner. Any questions?"

"No, sir."

"Richard, do you know why you're here?"

"Yes, sir."

"Tell me."

"For breakin' into the gym."

"Can you think of any other reason?"

"No." His tone was sullen again, and I noticed I wasn't "sir" any more.

"Why were you in the basement, Richard?" Estelle asked. Her voice was soft and silky, and the VU barely twitched.

We waited a full minute while Richard Staples examined the cuticle of his left index finger. A little sound that might have been a sniffle or just a noisy inhale told me that he hadn't fallen asleep.

"You weren't hiding from us, were you," Estelle said. I half expected Staples to say, "*Hell, who would?*" but he didn't. He raised his eyes from his cuticle to meet Estelle's gaze.

"Richard, we need answers that the recorder can hear," I prompted. Estelle had him locked in, but I wanted the kid to remember that there were other people in the room...and some of them nowhere near as kindly as the young lady.

"No, I wasn't hidin' from you," he said finally.

"Who from, then?"

I saw his jaw tighten and he went back to his cuticle again.

"Has someone threatened you?" Estelle asked.

"I ain't afraid of nobody," Richard Staples said without hesitation.

"I wouldn't think so," Estelle said. "But you said you weren't hiding from us. Will you tell us from whom, then?"

He lost interest in his finger and looked off toward the far corner of the ceiling. If he started counting ceiling tiles, we were going to be there all night.

"Richard, what can you tell us about the burglary at Wayne's Farm Supply last week?" Deputy Torrez said. I tried hard not to grin. His timing was perfect, dropping another bomb in the kid's lap just when he thought he could bore us more than we bored him.

Staples's eyes shifted to the table in front of him and he blinked hard.

While he was waiting, Deputy Torrez reached down and lifted his briefcase to the table. He opened it and shuffled papers for a few seconds before selecting the one that had been on top all along. He read it over before laying it on the table in front of him.

"We have information that two male subjects entered the back of the Wayne Supply building sometime between six p.m. Tuesday night and eight a.m. Wednesday morning of last week."

Torrez looked up and folded his large hands in front of him on the table like a priest about to say blessing for dinner. "We have evidence that tells us what size and brand of shoes one of the suspects wore. We have several sets of fingerprints lifted from the scene. We have a full inventory of goods taken from the scene. Several of the larger tools have not only serial numbers for identification but also the owner's identification number."

He paused a moment and regarded Richard Staples with interest. Staples squirmed in his chair and then turned slightly so he could rest his elbow on the table and his chin in his hand.

"We haven't fingerprinted you yet, but we'll have plenty of time for that after your arraignment," Torrez continued. "You want to talk to us about that burglary?" Torrez asked.

"I thought this was about the school," Staples said and even I almost felt sorry for the simple son of a bitch.

"Well, it could be about that too," Robert said easily. "But what we've also got is a statement from another party that links you to that burglary. And we do know, Richard, that there are ties to other residential burglaries in the area as well. We're talking eight or ten counts."

Even Richard Staples could count from one to two to ten, and before he had a chance to add up his chances, I said, "Where did you get the school keys, Richard?"

He frowned, thinking hard and fast. "I found 'em," he said without looking at me.

I nodded solemnly, as if I believed that yarn. I examined my little note pad for a full minute. "So tell me about Todd Sloan, Richard."

The kid's head snapped around to me so fast I thought I heard his bones pop.

"I didn't have nothin' to do with that," he said, and damned if there wasn't a hint of a quaver in his voice.

I leaned back in my chair and my hand fumbled around in my shirt pocket for the cigarette I didn't have. "Nothing to do with what, Richard?"

"Nothin' to do with him, I mean."

"But you know who he is?"

"Course I do."

"And you heard about what happened yesterday?"

"Yes. Everybody in town's talking about it."

"Richard," I said, "We have information that you associated with Todd Sloan on a routine basis at school and outside of school as well."

"That ain't true," Staples almost shouted. His right eye crinkled shut like he had dust in it. He rubbed it with his right index knuckle. "That ain't true. I didn't hang around with that little shit at all. There ain't no way I had anything to do with him gettin' killed."

Martin Holman had been leaning back in his chair with his arms crossed over his chest. He let his chair thump down and he leaned forward. I said a quick, silent prayer.

"Richard, you know, then, that we're actually investigating a double homicide." I breathed a sigh of relief. Holman knew that if we kept stacking, eventually Richard Staples's shell would crack. Just like breaking down a customer until he bought the used Oldsmobile.

This time, it wasn't a quaver in his voice. Staples's eyes went wide with pure panic. Any eighteen-year-old fool knows how much of his life could be spent in prison on a double homicide rap.

"Now lookit. I didn't have nothin' to do with any of that," he said.

"But you know who did," Estelle said. Her black, smoldering eyes must have bored into Richard Staples's brain. My pulse crept up a dozen notches. "Make it easy on yourself, Richard."

"This is deep, deep trouble, son," Holman murmured.

Richard Staples frowned hard, his head down. His lower lip twitched once, jutting out a bit and then jerking back in like he'd given something away. And then, almost in slow motion, he caved in until his head was resting on his crossed arms on the table. None of us moved or said anything.

After a full two minutes, the tape recorder clicked and I reached forward, snapped the eject, flipped the tape, closed the cover, and pressed record/play again.

"We're ready when you are, Richard," I said gently.

Richard Staples pushed himself upright and wiped at his right eye again. When he chose to speak, he was looking at Martin Holman. Damned if the sheriff hadn't made the sale.

30

"I ain't going to take the blame for no burglaries and then have him turn around and get away with what he done," Richard Staples said.

"Who are you talking about, Richard?" I asked.

"Kenny. He ain't puttin' the blame for everything on me."

"Kenny who, Richard?" Deputy Torrez prompted.

"Kenny Trujillo." None of us had mentioned Trujillo's name to Staples and I glanced at the tape player to make sure the gadget was still spinning.

"Richard, is it true that you worked a time or two out at Florek's wrecking yard? With Kenny Trujillo?"

"Yeah, I been there," Staples said. "I was thinkin' of workin' out there full time, startin' this summer."

Robert Torrez pulled a manila envelope from his briefcase. He shook several instant photos from the envelope into his hand, selected one, and slid it across the table to Staples.

"Is this the engine hoist that was stolen from Wayne's Farm Supply?"

Staples glanced at the photo carelessly. "Yeah, that's the one *he* took, not me."

Torrez retrieved the photo and handed it to me, knowing that I was waiting. The photo showed a chain hoist resting amid a sea of other automotive detritus on a grease-covered workbench. A tag attached to the bottom of the photo gave the date and time the photo was taken, along with the description: chain hoist, sn567901, Florek Auto Wrecking.

I handed the photo back to Torrez. I wasn't interested in hardware.

"You started to tell us what Trujillo was blaming you for," I said. "As it is, he says you were involved with Todd Sloan in several of the burglaries."

Staples shook his head. He leaned forward, his arms on the table, and held his hands about a basketball apart, as if to say "This is the way it is."

"Todd Sloan didn't have a damn thing to do with any of them burglaries," Staples said.

"Is that a fact."

"Yes, sir. Me and Kenny did."

"We know that," I said, not adding the *now* that would tell Staples how much of a wrong tree we'd been barking up...unless this simple son of a bitch was lying as effortlessly as breathing.

I took the plunge. "Who killed Todd Sloan, Richard?"

"Kenny Trujillo and his mom."

"I beg your pardon?"

"Kenny and Todd's mom. Miriam Sloan."

"They both did it?"

"Yes, sir."

The room was so quiet we could hear the roaches breathing. "Tell us," I said.

"Okay, see—" Richard Staples pawed around for a good starting place. "Todd hated Kenny's guts." He managed a ghost of a smile. "More than he hated mine, I guess. I hung around out there some, 'cause of what Kenny and me was doin'. But Todd?" He shook his head with disdain. "We sure weren't friends. No sir. But he sure didn't like Trujillo."

"Was he jealous?"

"What do you mean?"

"I mean," I said slowly, "did Todd dislike Kenny because Trujillo was Miriam Sloan's live-in boyfriend?"

"Yeah, that," Staples said. "I guess that was it, mostly. Todd was all the time talking about how great his old man was, the one who moved to Florida. Him and Kenny'd get into these arguments, and once Kenny smacked him clear across the room. I thought it was kinda funny, myself. The little shit had it comin'." Staples looked up quickly. "Bein' hit, I mean."

"And then?"

"Well, things got worse and worse, far as I could see. Course, I didn't care much. Kenny and me was doin' all right. But I was there one night when Todd didn't leave...he usually did that, you know, when Kenny came home. Got so the two of them couldn't be in that trailer at the same time without a fight startin'. Anyways, about two weeks ago, Todd comes up with this thing that he's going to turn both Kenny and his mom in to the welfare department for somethin'...I don't remember."

"Welfare fraud?" Estelle prompted.

Staples nodded vigorously. "That was it. Yep. He kept sayin' that with what Kenny made down to the wreckin' yard and what his mom made workin' part time, they didn't qualify for all they was gettin'. Kenny told him that if he said anything he'd fry him for sure. That was the night he smacked him a good lick."

"What happened the day Todd was killed, Richard?"

"We just come back from messin' around downtown, and Todd was there. We was showin' Miriam what all we had—"

"Are you talking about what you got in a burglary?"

Staples nodded again. "Yeah. Anyways, Todd went off on this thing about how we was going to get everyone in trouble. He kept sayin' like how Kenny just wanted his mom in jail so he could have the trailer and all." I glanced at Estelle. These boys set their sights high, I thought.

"And then he got off on that welfare shit again, how he was goin' to cut 'em all off and send 'em to jail. I guess Kenny just had all he could take."

"What happened?"

Staples coughed and Holman said, "You want a soda or something?"

"You got a cigarette?"

"No, but we can get you some. We'll take a break in a few minutes."

"What did Trujillo do then?" I asked, irritated at the interruption.

"He had this little revolver, this little twenty-two? He had it in his coat pocket. He pulled it out and shoved it in Todd's stomach and pulled the trigger. Right there in the living room of the trailer.

Todd, he'd been gettin' up when he saw Kenny comin', and he fell right over the arm of the chair."

Richard Staples stopped talking and stared down at the table again, picking at his nails. "Kenny got this real funny look on his face, like he was surprised he'd shot Todd, and now what was he going to do. Cause Todd was all curled up on the floor, holdin' his gut and hollerin' like a stuck pig."

"You said his mother was involved. What did she do?"

"We all just sat there, not knowin' what to do, with Todd layin' on the floor, screamin' and swearin' at us, sayin' all the things he was gonna do. And Miriam just looks down at him all cold and fishy like and says to Kenny, 'Kenny, don't just let him lie there like that. Make him stop.' That's what she said. 'Make him stop.'" Staples bit his lip.

"And he did, too. He got up and put that little gun right behind Todd's left ear and he shoots him again. *Pow.* Just like that."

I took a deep breath. "And then you buried him."

"Shit, I was so fuckin' scared I damn near shit my pants."

"I bet."

"See, I didn't know what Kenny was going to do with that gun in his hand. I figure it'd be as easy for him to use it on me as not, bein' I saw the whole thing. He kinda had a crazy look on his face like he was thinkin', 'I gone and done it now and what the hell, it wasn't all that big a deal.' Scared the shit out of me."

"So what did you do," Estelle prompted.

"Kenny says, 'We got to bury him,' and Miriam says, 'Where? You can't let no one see you.' And Kenny decides that right behind the trailer, in that old pasture, is just fine, cause nobody ever goes there. So he tells me to grab the kid's feet, and I do, and we carry him outside."

"When was this?" I asked.

"Friday night."

"What time? Late? When?"

"I don't know. Maybe eight, nine o'clock. Somethin' like that. And then we set to diggin' just on the other side of the fence, where it's real soft and sandy. I did most of the diggin'. Kenny just kept sayin' 'Deeper,' or 'Over there more,' or 'Make it longer.' I was real tempted to put that shovel up his ass, but he had that gun all the time. I just did as I was told."

"Smart man," Torrez said.

"Yeah. And then I about fainted cause Todd made a noise and I dropped the shovel and Kenny he jerks around and shoots with that little gun again. I don't know if he hit him or not, but I couldn't believe he done that. It sounded so damn loud outside like that. Miriam, she heard the shot, all right, and she comes out to see what's goin' on. We was set to put the body in the hole and I said, 'What if he ain't dead?' Kenny, he says, 'He's dead all right. Put 'im in the hole.' And so I did. And I guess then he was dead all right."

"And that's all?" I asked.

"Well, Miriam, she had a light, and she held it to make sure that we had the hole all filled and covered smooth so no one could tell. We was about done but she was lookin' at something else, cause the light was wanderin' so it was hard to see. I was going to say somethin' about holdin' the light still when she says, 'She's watchin'.'"

"Who was watching?" Estelle asked, but with a deep, certain dread, I already knew the answer.

"That old lady across the field. We stopped what we was doin' and Miriam turned off the light. We could see the old lady standin' on the back porch, with the light comin' out the door behind her. Kinda lit her up, just enough so we could see her."

"Are you talking about Mrs. Hocking? Anna Hocking?"

"Yes, sir. Miriam says, 'She heard the shot.' I said, 'She couldn't have. She couldn't see what we're doin'.' And Miriam says real quiet like, 'I'm not taking the chance that she might call the police.' That's all she said."

I slumped back in my chair. "And so Miriam Sloan went over to Anna Hocking's house?"

"That's what she did. And *that* scared the livin' shit out of me, too…not so much right then, cause I didn't know what to think, but later on that night, when every cop in five counties was there, shit."

"When was the body moved?" Estelle asked. She spoke so quietly even Richard Staples's good teenage hearing didn't catch it.

"Excuse me?" Staples was now completely comfortable in his new role as Mr. Cooperation.

"When was the body moved?" Estelle repeated. If Staples expected sympathy from her, he was mistaken. Her face was like carved marble, too pale now with suppressed anger.

"We all split, knowin' that the cops would be by to talk with anybody in the neighborhood. Miriam, she said she made it look just like an accident, and not to worry. But Kenny, he was spooked, you know? He was sure they'd bring dogs. That's all he could talk about. So right after dark the next night, we saw things was pretty quiet. Kenny, he handed me the shovel and I dug Todd up and we wrapped him in a piece of plastic that Kenny stole from the wreckin' yard.

"Then we put the body in the back of Kenny's truck, and covered it with a bunch of old tires. Then we drove out to that old crazy man's place."

"Richard," I said, "tell me something. How was it you chose that spot? With all the other places in the county you could have chosen?"

Staples made a wry face. "That was Kenny's brilliant idea. He said he'd been out that road a while back, and saw the old man workin', buryin' something. Kenny said no one dared mess with the old man's property, cause he'd as soon shoot you between the eyes as look at you. So he got this bee in his head that that would be the perfect spot."

"And so you went out there."

"Yep. We could see the spot, just like Kenny said. The fresh dirt and all. There was even this little cross made out of two sticks tied together. Kenny pulled it out of the ground and says, 'Old Todd don't need this to go to hell.' We dug down and saw it was three dogs that he'd buried. And Kenny gets this great idea. 'Ain't no one ever going to figure this out,' he says. And he makes me dig to hell and gone deeper, figurin' to bury Todd and put the dogs on top of him. It woulda worked, 'cept this other old fart comes along, sees our light, and comes over, wantin' to know what we're doing on his land."

"Stuart Torkelson."

"I guess. Kenny, he tries to sweet-talk the guy, tellin' him about these dogs that we was buryin' for the old man who lives in the woods up there. I'm tryin' to block the hole, 'cause there's parts of Todd Sloan stickin' out, even though there's plastic coverin' most of him. This guy, he didn't buy it, and he pushes past me and looks in the hole. He swings around and Kenny, he shoots him clean through with this huge old magnum he stole from some place last summer.

"And the old guy screams and spins like a top, landin' right on top of one of them dead dogs. But he sure surprised me when he stumbles to his feet and starts down toward the road. He fell a couple times and then Kenny caught up with him and shoots him again in the head."

Richard Staples stopped talking like someone had shoved a cork down his throat. His jaw worked a couple of times, and then the energy that he'd been using to hold himself together ran out. He hung his head and gulped great lungfuls of air until I was afraid he was going to hyperventilate. He threw his head back so hard it cracked the back of the old chair. He didn't notice. He was clenching his eyes closed, determined not to let us see him cry.

"Jesus, what's going to happen to me," he managed.

I tried to keep my tone sincere and kindly. "Absolutely nothing, Richard, assuming you're telling us the truth. Nothing, compared to what's going to happen to Kenny Trujillo and Miriam Sloan."

"He made me pull the plastic around real tight and then bury Todd. And then he had this idea about fillin' in part of the hole with rocks. He said no one would ever dig past them. And all this time, I'm worryin' about that dead body, lyin' down in the field. But old Kenny, he had an answer for everything. 'They'll just blame the old Mexican for it, like always,' he says."

"And you believed him," I said. "Until you heard that we'd found Sloan's body. And then you figured that you were the only witness. You were waiting for Kenny Trujillo to come knocking on your door, weren't you?"

Staples nodded. "I was going to wait until dark, and then steal my aunt's car. I was going to split, man."

"Where to?"

"It don't matter. But I know Kenny...he's crazy. He'd make sure I couldn't talk to no one."

"When you saw us, why didn't you just come and talk to us?"

Staples looked at me as if I were nuts, as if the simplest solution were the most bizarre.

"All right, Richard, thank you. We'll be talking lots more, be prepared for that." Staples looked resigned...and relieved. "You understand that we have to hold you in protective custody for a while, don't you?"

"Yes, sir."

"One last thing." I tore off a clean sheet of paper from the pad in front of me. I drew a rough sketch of the Sloan trailer and its location in the Paradise View Trailer Park. "Put an X where you dug the first grave," I said.

Richard Staples scrutinized the drawing. "It'd be right here along the fence line, right opposite the kitchen window," he said.

"You're sure?"

"Positive. I ain't about to forget."

How thoughtful Miriam Sloan had been, choosing a spot where she could watch the morning sun come up over her son's grave while she fixed bacon and eggs for her boyfriend.

31

Estelle Reyes-Guzman was furious with me in her own quiet way. I refused to let her ride along on the bust. She offered fifteen good reasons why she should go, and I countered with one single stubborn response.

"No," I said. "It's not worth risking your hide for the likes of these people." I handed her the keys to my Blazer. "Go home and fix dinner for Francis One and Two." When she started to protest again, I added, "And then go over to the hospital and spend the evening with Reuben. He needs you. These creeps don't. I'll be along when this is all wrapped up."

And it might have been wrapped up neatly, too, if Deputy Eddie Mitchell had stayed in his patrol car.

Just as I was coming down the stairway behind Sheriff Holman, I heard Mitchell's calm voice coming over the radio in the dispatch room.

"PCS, three zero six."

"Go ahead, three oh six," Tony Abeyta replied.

"PCS, one male subject has left the trailer and is heading for his truck."

I shoved past Holman and barged into the dispatch room, damn near running over Mrs. Perna. "Three zero six, that subject is armed and extremely dangerous. You let him leave and then stick to his tail."

"Ten four, PCS."

"And three zero two, do you copy?"

"Ten four, PCS," Paul Encinos replied instantly.

"Three zero two, don't take your eyes off that trailer."

"Ten four, PCS."

Bob Torrez was already out the door, and I could hear the bellow of his patrol car as it charged out of the parking lot. I grabbed the keys to 310 off the board and pushed my waddle up to as close to a sprint as I could out the door. I didn't expect Martin Holman to follow, but he did and I damn near ripped his legs off as I pulled the car into reverse to back out of the slot.

"Jesus, Bill, wait until I'm in the damn car," he cried.

"Sorry. We're kind of in a hurry here." I picked up the mike just as Paul Encinos's frantic voice shot over the airwaves.

"PCS, officer is down. I think he's—" and the transmission stopped.

The taillights of Bob Torrez's patrol car were already out of sight and I accelerated down the center of Bustos Avenue with Martin holding onto the door grip. A station wagon edged out of a side street and poked its nose halfway out into the avenue before the driver woke up and judged that I was trying for escape velocity. He locked his brakes as I shot past.

Holman reached down and hit the switches for the lights and siren.

"Thanks," I said, and we slid, tires howling, around the sweeping turn that was the eastbound intersection with Camino del Sol.

"PCS, he's heading toward town on County Road Nineteen," Paul Encinos said, and I felt a surge of relief hearing his voice. "I've lost him."

"Three zero eight, he should be coming up on you then. Can you block him off?" I dropped the mike in Martin's lap as we shot across the cattle guard that marked the end of pavement and the beginning of gravel. I squinted into the gathering darkness ahead, trying to see lights.

"I'll see what I can do," Torrez said, and he sounded as if he'd been asked to baste the barbecued chicken at a church picnic. We crested a rise and I saw the bright flash of Torrez's roof lights as they pulsed across the arroyo. Dancing toward him was a set of headlights, bobbing and weaving crazily.

I damn near lost it on the curve past Valerio's Mobile Home Park and for a second I had a vision of the sheriff and me sailing through the old drive-in movie screen. The curve blocked my view of the lights ahead but the radio crackled again.

"Well, that didn't work," Torrez's voice said calmly. "Three ten, he's comin' at you." I made a quick decision and pumped the brakes to pull down to a near stop on the loose gravel.

"You going to block the road?" Holman shouted. His legs were stiff against the firewall. If he pushed any harder he'd break the seatback and end up in the trunk.

"No." I pulled wide of the road and spun 310 around in the gravel, then lurched to a stop. The headlights of the oncoming vehicle stabbed around the bend and then washed over us. I saw Martin Holman tense, both hands grabbing for the door handle.

I was parked well off the road, though, and the driver would have had to make a deliberate effort to hit us. He'd taken out two or three cars already, I guessed. Bashing 310 would leave the department on foot.

Kenny Trujillo saw that he was being offered an opening and he poured the coals to it. The yellow pickup went by in a cloud of dust and flying gravel. It was too dark to see, but I could imagine the smile of triumph wiped all over his grimy face.

And then County Road 19 managed to do what we couldn't. I hoped that Anna Hocking was able to look down from her patch of heaven and watch the action. She wouldn't gloat, of course. She'd been too much of a grand old lady to do that. But she surely would have allowed herself a little twinge of grim satisfaction.

Just about the time the back tires of 310 clawed enough traction to put us in pursuit, Kenny Trujillo overcooked it. The thrill of being offered an open door canceled out any cool-headed judgment he may have had left. We heard the bellow of the pickup's V-8, and even as I accelerated the patrol car back onto 19, I saw the truck's one taillight up ahead waltz first one way and then another as the bald tires fought for traction. Trujillo tried to force it around the curve by the drive-in but it didn't work.

The long, slow slide was almost graceful, marked by the red glow of the taillight as it arced far to the left and then snapped back to the right. The pickup charged across the road, plunged down into the ditch and rocketed back out to re-cross the county road. There wasn't much on the other side, as Abe Hocking had discovered briefly fifty years before.

My own headlights and the side spot caught a flash of yellow metal as Kenny Trujillo's pickup truck catapulted off the edge of Arroyo del Cerdo at close to eighty miles an hour. The drop wasn't spectacular, just enough to ensure that the Ford's nose would be pointed down at a perfect forty-five degree angle when it hit the sandy arroyo bottom.

I slid 310 to a stop at the lip of the arroyo. If the pickup's one taillight was still burning, it was dug too far into the sand to see. Martin Holman's door flew open but I stabbed out an arm and grabbed him before he could leap out of the car.

"Don't go running down there," I snapped. Holman looked at me with his eyes as big as saucers. A person's first eyewitnessed crash is always an attention-getter, even if it's at night and all you saw was a spectacular light show. After about a dozen, they're all the same—twisted metal with ugly things inside. "If he isn't unconscious and still has a gun, you'll be the one lying dead in the bottom of that arroyo."

"He's got to be dead," Holman stammered.

"No loss," I said and Holman grimaced. "But I've seen 'em walk away from ones much worse than that." I glanced in the rearview mirror as Bob Torrez idled up behind us, the flashing lights on his car's roof looking like a carnival ride.

I keyed the mike. "Three zero eight…"

Torrez clicked the mike switch to tell me he was listening.

"Go check on Encinos and Mitchell, and if they're all right, go arrest the second half. Be careful."

"Ten four." The patrol car backed up, turned around and kicked gravel as Torrez headed toward the Paradise View Trailer Park.

I pressed the electric lock that released the shotgun. "Let's go see," I said. And then I stopped and looked at Holman. "Do you have anything that shoots?"

Damned if he didn't blush. "Ah, no."

I sighed and pulled out my own .357. "Take this."

It would have been a real chore climbing down into the arroyo in any case, but the loose footing in the deepening December darkness was enough to make me want to wait and talk with Kenny Trujillo's remains in the morning. I twisted the spotlight so the glare picked up the arroyo's rim. The pickup truck had caved in the top lip of the sand bank when it plunged over.

I stepped to the edge and swung my flashlight back and forth, looking for the best route down. The choices were slim. I slid down the twenty feet, trying to avoid the cacti still clinging bravely to the arroyo banks. Holman followed, his movements irritatingly effortless and graceful as always.

I reached the bottom of the arroyo and stopped, the wreck's carcass thirty feet ahead. The only sounds from the pickup truck were gentle pinging sounds as the hot metal cooled. I swept the light across the scrap pile, looking for movement.

A load of junk that had been in the bed of the truck for decades had cascaded past the cab when it landed. Chunks of concrete, a rim for a tractor tire, old tools, a handyman jack…all had sprayed forward, much of it crashing through the truck's back window.

The frame had buckled as the body of the truck folded and the engine drove off its mounts backward into the cab. The deep gouges in the sandy arroyo bottom indicated that the pickup had pitched end over end twice. It had come to rest upside down in a tangle of bent and rusted metal.

I circled the truck and saw an elbow sticking out through where the windshield had been. The elbow wasn't moving. With the shotgun and flashlight preceding me, I bent down so I could see into the cab.

The crash had taken the fight out of Kenny Trujillo. He was crammed between the crumpled steering wheel and the dashboard. From the blood smeared on the passenger's side, I could see that he'd been thrown hard against the right side windshield post and then, as the truck rolled, he'd been pitched back to the left, where the truck had clamped him solidly.

With a grunt I knelt down, reached through the side window, and felt for a pulse. There was a faint one, fluttering and erratic.

Kenny Trujillo's head was twisted in the small space left between the roof and the dash, his left cheek about where the bottom windshield track used to be. And even while I held his wrist, the pulse flickered, stumbled, and then stopped.

I pulled away and stood up. "What do you think?" Holman asked. He didn't want to step too close.

"I think he's dead," I said. I started back toward the arroyo bank.

"What about him?" Holman called after me.

"He'll keep." The struggle up the bank cost me dearly, and for a long moment I had to sit in the patrol car until the black spots stopped dancing before my eyes and my pulse returned to normal. By then Martin Holman, not even breathing hard, was in the car.

"You want me to call for the coroner and the wrecker?" he asked, ever helpful.

I took a deep breath. "Yeah, go ahead." I listened to him talk to the dispatcher. I don't know why I was surprised that the sheriff was doing a decent job. It gave me a minute to think. I wanted nothing more than to charge down the road and assist Bob Torrez and the others, but someone needed to stay with the wrecked truck. I had just the man.

When he was finished, I jerked a thumb toward the mess down in the arroyo. "Will you stay here until I can break someone else free?"

"Well, sure," Holman said. He started to open the door and hesitated, looking uncertain. "Well sure," he said again as if he had convinced himself. I left him there, standing in the dark with a flashlight and my .357 for company.

From the old drive-in theater to the Paradise Trailer Park was 1.7 miles, and it seemed like two hundred. I rounded the last sweeping curve and backed off. The road was nearly blocked with junk that had once been half of Posadas County's patrol car fleet. The sight would have kept Holman babbling about budget for hours.

Torrez had pulled up directly behind Mrs. Sloan's Oldsmobile, the light from his spotlight concentrated beyond on the trailer's front door. Half in the trailer park's driveway and half in the county road was Eddie Mitchell's patrol car, its left front door, fender and wheel crumpled and jammed.

Thirty yards down the road sat Deputy Encinos's Ford, its front end so crushed that the radiator would be wrapped around the front of the engine block. The hood was buckled so badly that even if the old thing had had the gumption to run, the driver wouldn't have been able to see the road.

I blocked the rest of the driveway and got out of the car. Eddie Mitchell was sitting in the sand just out of the headlights' glare, leaning against the rough trunk of a stunted juniper seedling that grew beside the trailer park's collection of mailboxes.

I swept my flashlight up enough to see his pale face. He was hurting—and disgusted. "They're right over there," he said, pointing. I turned and looked. Deputy Torrez and Deputy Encino were escorting Miriam Sloan through the weeds from the direction of Ulibarri's trailer. As they approached Torrez's car, I could see that her hands were cuffed behind her back. With a deputy at each elbow, she had shrunk from stout and blustery to pathetic.

"She was trying to run up that way after the kid took off," Eddie said.

"What happened to you?"

"Busted my ankle. He damn near punted me clear across the road," Mitchell said ruefully. "And then he stopped, bam, and backed up full speed right into Paul. He stalled it, and for a minute I thought he was going to get out. I guess Paul was stunned or something, cause he didn't get out of his car right away."

"Probably a damn good thing he didn't."

"That son of a bitch got the truck going again and had to ram into the car a couple times to get his bumper loose. I couldn't get out my door, and by the time I squirmed across the seat, he was gone. I tried one shot as he went by, but didn't hit anything."

I knelt down and looked at the deputy's left ankle, now ballooning and crooked. "You want me to cut your boot off?" I said, and that fetched a look of panic.

"No, sir. I sure don't," he said.

"The EMTs will be here in just a few minutes," I said. I watched as Torrez and Encinos deposited Miriam Sloan in the back of Torrez's car. I had no desire to talk with the woman. Looking at her in court was going to be enough of a punishment.

32

By nine-thirty that evening our procedure was organized enough that each one of the deputies could work for a week nonstop. Bob Torrez was almost gleeful at the prospect of wrapping up nearly a dozen burglaries with one sweep. Sheriff Martin Holman was doubly perturbed—his house fire and break-in were not on the list, and half of his county fleet had been put in dry dock.

I broke away shortly before ten and started to dial Estelle. I had touched the first three numbers before I thought better of it. I didn't want the phone jangling to wake the kid—or his parents for that matter.

I called Posadas General Hospital instead and checked with the nurses' desk. Evelyn Bistoff was on duty and she told me that the Guzmans had spent most of the evening with old Reuben and then left the hospital at nine. Reuben was holding his own.

As the deputies started to tear the Sloans' trailer apart, I felt confident enough to call Linda Rael into my office. The young lady was dragging but game…I admired her persistence. And this time, when she asked questions I gave her all the information we had. I knew that on several items I might be jumping the gun, but I wanted her—and her paper—to beat out all the big city, high pressure outfits.

The Sloans' trailer revealed enough immediate evidence to corroborate Richard Staples's story. Miriam Sloan had tried to sponge out most of a blood stain in the center of the living room rug, right beside the coffee table. The stain, spread to a circle of nearly a yard's diameter, was covered with a cheap throw rug that still stank of polyester newness.

Early the next morning, deputies Paul Encinos and Tony Abeyta would play prospector, taking Staples's map and excavating the first grave that had held Todd Sloan. Enough of his blood would have seeped into the sand that it would be significant evidence for the medical examiner.

Miriam Sloan hadn't conned enough money out of the Department of Social Services to be able to afford to pay a lawyer, and Dean Ontiveros, the public defender, wouldn't be back from a Las Cruces trial until late afternoon. The woman refused to say a word without Ontiveros present, so there she sat in one of our cells, sullen and trapped. Ontiveros was going to have a good time with her. If he was smart, he'd stay in Las Cruces.

By midnight we were organized and caught up with paperwork enough so that we could see the general flow of the case. And I was running on fumes.

I pushed back from my desk, shoving my reading glasses up into my crewcut and rubbing my eyes. I hoped that no one would walk through the door for the next five minutes. Given that head start, I could work up enough gumption to get up out of my chair and head for home.

There was nothing wrong with me that fifty hours of sleep and five thousand calories of food wouldn't cure. The sleep would come in fifteen minute bursts during the next month...and maybe Estelle, Francis, and the kid would consider being treated to a middle-of-the-night dinner of Mexican food so hot it would ignite gasoline.

Sheriff Martin Holman startled me out of my trance. He'd been working the burglary list that Richard Staples had turned over to Bob Torrez, hoping something would show up. I think he would have been satisfied to discover just his Toro rototiller.

"I didn't get a chance to tell you," he said by way of introduction. I opened one eye and groaned. He thought I was just tired. I was groaning at the prospect of a mea culpa confession.

"I was impressed with the way the deputies handled all this."

I nodded and waited, my hands hooked behind my head.

Holman eased forward into my office and hooked the door closed with his toe. "I felt a little bit foolish out there," he said.

"Why would that be?" I asked. "You did what needed to be done."

He smiled at that and sat down in the chair at the end of my desk. I was beginning to feel like a priest at confession. "What do you think?" he asked. "I mean, really?"

"About what?"

"About the way things are going." He was looking at the top of my desk instead of eye to eye. I knew what he wanted to ask.

"Martin," I said and let my chair swing forward with a loud squeak as I pulled my arms down. I folded my hands in the middle of my desk pad and looked at him with a mixture of amusement and respect. "Let me tell you something." His eyes flicked up to mine and I could see a little apprehension there.

"We need good administration at the top. Any organization does. And we've got it. I know you're not a cop, and I know that that bothers you from time to time. But I don't think you really want to be, either. You seem to have an instinct about when to step back and stay out of the way." He sighed with relief. "We've had a better budget, and better relations with the county commission, and better, more sensible cost management in the last three years than I can ever remember."

"I appreciate hearing that."

"Just concentrate on what you're good at, Martin. Over time, you'll catch on to the rest. Are you going to the FBI school this spring?"

"I might. I don't know. But I've been thinking about it."

"It'd be good for you." I looked at my watch. "I need to check on Reuben Fuentes again. Is there anything else you need in the next little while?"

He flashed his best used car salesman's smile. "You'd know that better than I."

"Then I'm going home for a little bit."

As I stood up, Holman opened my office door and asked, "Now that you're in over your head with all this paperwork, what are you going to do about the christening you were planning to attend down in Tres Santos?"

I shrugged. "That's something else hanging," I said.

I walked through the front door of my home at seventeen minutes after midnight. The place was stone quiet and dark except for a single light that filtered out into the hall from my living room.

I hung my Stetson on the ugly hatrack behind the door. I'd bought the rack in a moment of weakness during the auction at the old Ortiz Hotel over in San Pasquale.

Estelle Reyes-Guzman was curled up on the sofa in the living room. She was wrapped in one of my bathrobes and it was a tent that would have covered five of her. She wasn't watching *The Shootist*. The tube was dead. She was leafing through one of my ten-year-old copies of *New Mexico Magazine*.

"Welcome home, *Padrino*," she said.

"Hey," I replied. "Why are you still up?"

She ignored my question, a habit of hers that I liked to think she'd learned from me years before. "I listened to your scanner some," she said. "Quite a chase you had."

I shrugged. "The Trujillo kid tried to run and over-cooked it into the arroyo. Bob got the woman without any problems, though." As far as I was concerned, Miriam Sloan was as much history as her pathetic boyfriend. Estelle correctly read my thoughts and changed the subject.

"We visited Uncle Reuben earlier this evening."

"I know. I called the hospital. The nurse said you'd been there."

"He seems so at peace."

"I hope so."

Estelle patted the cushion beside her and I sat down with a popping of knees and the creak of gunbelt leather. I wasn't sure I'd be able to get back up.

"What would you think of having the christening here?"

"I beg your pardon?"

She smiled at the startled expression on my face. "This is what I was thinking—" and she ticked off the points on her fingers. "Number one, you're too busy right now to get away for any length of time. Number two, I can't leave Uncle Reuben alone now. Three, Francis can drive down to Tres Santos, pick up mama, and be back here in two hours."

She stopped counting. "Uncle Reuben isn't taking medications any more and Francis said he would bring him here if you were willing. He and I could do as much for Uncle Reuben here as he's getting in the hospital. That way, he'd be with us." Thinking I might mind, she added quickly, "Just for the ceremony, sir."

"Estelle," I said, laying a hand on hers, "I've told you before. This house is yours. *Mi casa*...something something *casa*, or however that saying goes."

"*Mi casa es su casa.*"

"Right. The saying means just what it says. If you want to have your mother up here, and Reuben, and whoever else, then have at it."

"You wouldn't mind? Francis said we were asking too much, and I guess we are."

I grinned at her. "Hey, if I mind, I can always get in three-ten and go do some work, right?"

"And you would, too."

"You're going to invite the Diaz family up? Your mother's neighbors?"

"There are twelve of them, sir."

"So what? I've got five acres, five bedrooms. There's a motel just five blocks away if we need it. Reuben will have a live-in physician to keep him happy. He can swap lies with your mother until all hours. It'll be fun."

Estelle made a funny face and then reached over to hug me...or as close as someone could come to a hug around someone of my girth. She didn't let go right away and I knew she was well aware of the unspoken truth—that Reuben would be lucky to live through the next couple days, much less live through any sentimental conversations with his aging niece.

I pulled an arm free and looked at my watch.

"I've got to get some food," I said. "Do you suppose Tommy's Diner is still open? I haven't eaten dinner yet, for God's sake."

"Would you mind some company?"

"Not at all. Are the two Francises awake?"

"No." She stood up. "But I'll tell my husband. He's a light sleeper. I think they teach that in medical school."

"Get him to come along," I said.

"No." Estelle shook her head. "Just the two of us." She flashed me a smile as she vanished down the hall toward Camille's bedroom.

In five minutes she was back, dressed in jeans and sweatshirt, looking more like the middle of a spring morning than the dark of a December midnight.

I was too tired to bother with changing. Outside, I felt the chill of the air for the first time that day. The county car was parked askew in my driveway, blocking both my Blazer and the Guzmans' Isuzu.

"What the hell, we'll take three-ten," I said. "I've spent so much time in it the past twelve hours it feels like home."

I started the engine and just as the big V-8 burbled into life, the radio barked a message. I ignored it but Estelle didn't. She reached down and turned off the radio. The dashboard looked oddly blank without the dumb little amber light staring me in the face.

I laughed. "All right," I said. "It's a deal. Just this once."

To receive a free catalog of other Poisoned Pen Press titles, please
contact us in one of the following ways:

Phone: 1-800-421-3976
Facsimile: 1-480-949-1707
Email: info@poisonedpenpress.com
Website: www.poisonedpenpress.com

Poisoned Pen Press
6962 E. First Ave. Ste 103
Scottsdale, AZ 85251